The moon hung [...] Holiday rode into Miles City. It was late. He stopped at the Carlson House and checked in.

He followed Jedediah to a room. When Jed turned, Holiday held out a ten-dollar gold coin. "I'm lookin' for a man named Slade. He pass this way?"

Jed's eyes studied the muscular gunfighter, his dusty jeans, his lawman jacket. He saw the badge.

"Slade?"

"Yeah, Frank Slade," Holiday said, dropping the coin into Jedediah's hand. "Know anything about him?"

"Maybe."

Holiday waited. "Well?"

Jed knew he'd lose his job if he spilled his guts. He kept his hand out. Holiday deposited another coin.

"Slade, you say?"

"Get on with it," Holiday snapped.

"Frank Slade left here several days ago, headed west."

"Where's he going?"

"Can't say. Just know he rode west along the Yellowstone."

Holiday went to his room and locked the door. He lay back on the bed. His body ached. "I'm gettin' old," he mumbled. "Never hurt like this before, just from riding."

He dozed off. In the morning Holiday would get up and do fifty fast draws in the mirror.

A manhunter had to stay in shape.

Other books in the *Slade* series:

Days of '76

Link Pennington

SLADE

ESCAPE FROM MONTANA

LYNX BOOKS

New York

ESCAPE FROM MONTANA

ISBN: 1-55802-138-8

First Printing/February 1989

This is a work of fiction. Names, characters, places, and incidents are either the product of the author's imagination or are used fictitiously. Any resemblance to actual events, locales, or persons, living or dead, is entirely coincidental.

This book is published by Lynx Books, a division of Lynx Communications, Inc., 41 Madison Avenue, New York, New York, 10010. The name ''Lynx'' together with the logotype consisting of a stylized head of a lynx is a trademark of Lynx Communications, Inc.

Printed in the United States of America

0 9 8 7 6 5 4 3 2 1

Prologue
Dodge City, Kansas
Spring 1877

Cliff Langdon, rich, fat, famous, and now mayor of Dodge City, leaned back in his plush leather chair. He took a drink of expensive whiskey and drew a freckled finger along a jagged scar on his cheek.

"Frank Slade did this," he snarled.

Jubal Holiday sat across a big desk from Langdon, wearing a gray suit with red vest and black boots. He was lanky and handsome, his hair a wild frizz of blond curls that gave him a youthful look for a man of thirty-seven.

Langdon poured more whiskey into his shot glass, took a sip, and eyed Holiday. "Frank Slade did it. He ruined my face, robbed my bank, and killed a guard. If

I don't become governor of Kansas one day it'll be because of my face."

Holiday knew the story. Both versions. He'd heard how Langdon, the banker and land baron, had sent a gang of killers to steal old man Slade's land. After they'd shot Frank's mom and dad, young Slade had come blazing out of the barn with a rifle and gunned them all down, buried his parents, then disappeared for several years down into Texas. He'd worked the cattle trails. He'd practiced his fast draw. He'd polished his timing, then snuck back into Dodge City and paid Langdon a visit, leaving him with a face full of scars and $17,000 poorer.

Holiday had also heard Langdon's side of the story, that Slade was a common bank robber, how Slade had attacked Langdon one night in his bank, disfigured his face, killed a guard, and made off with the money.

Holiday didn't care which story was true. He was a hired gun. His services were for sale, and right now Cliff Langdon was buying.

"You want me to take him out, right?" Holiday said.

"Frank Slade," Langdon drawled. "I want the bastard dead or alive. I prefer you bring him in alive, of course, but dead's okay."

Holiday pulled a slim cheroot from inside his coat, struck a lucifer on the heel of his boot, and lit the cigar. "I understand."

"There's a big reward, twenty-five thousand dollars. I'll go higher if you bring him back alive." Langdon leaned into his desk, opened a drawer, and withdrew an envelope. "You come highly touted, Holiday. I understand there hasn't been a man you didn't get once you went after him."

Holiday smiled. "You heard right."

Langdon handed him the envelope. "Expense money. There's enough here to see you through. Last I heard about Frank Slade he was in Deadwood up in the Dakota Territory. I hired the Pueblo Kid last year, sent him after Slade. He didn't come back. I got his badge in the mail."

"Slade's most likely moved on by now," Holiday speculated.

Langdon sipped from his shot glass. "I'd say you're right about that."

"But I can pick up his trail in Deadwood."

Langdon threw a badge on the desk. "You've been appointed a federal marshal with one assignment . . . get Frank Slade." He handed a warrant to Holiday. "The governor gives you his blessing."

Holiday lifted the warrant, folded it carefully, and slipped it into his coat. "I know what Slade looks like. I can track him down."

Langdon pushed forward in his chair, leaned across his desk, and appraised Holiday. "Slade's a mean, ruthless, young killer. Bring him back alive. You'll get much more than the reward."

"I haven't failed yet," Holiday said, puffing confidently on his cheroot.

Langdon tipped the whiskey bottle and splashed a shot in Holiday's glass, then filled his own. He grinned and said, "That's precisely why I hired you, Mr. Holiday."

Chapter One

Frank Slade rode his big Appaloosa to the edge of a coulee. A blazing spring sun glared him straight in the eye. The desolate high country of Montana lifted in the distance, and the ribbon of trail he'd been riding out of Dakota stretched out behind him.

A shot rang out. A whistling slug of hot lead chipped a boulder near Slade. His Appaloosa reared and whinnied, and he tumbled out of the saddle clutching his Winchester rifle. He levered a shell into the chamber and raced to a cluster of rocks near the base of a colored butte.

Bullets spat dirt around him. He leapt the rocks and slammed down on his belly. He peeked over a boulder. In the distance, across the coulee, several men scrambled from their horses and ran for cover.

Slade pumped off three warning shots.

He received a quick answer. A sharp crack of rifle fire. The rocks pinged.

Slade waited. Wind whipped dust around him. Then a voice yelled, "You're surrounded! Throw down your guns!"

Slade rolled over and saw rifle barrels dipping over the edge of the butte.

"Aw, shit," he whispered, taking a deep breath. They had him. He was outmanned.

"Push the rifle and pistol away, and just stay layin' there on your belly like that."

Slade dropped the Winchester and laid his pistol off to the side, then waited, his mind rattling with confusion.

He had spent the winter north of Medora in the Dakota Territory hiding out with the Mandan Indians, a tribe that had always been at peace with the white man. Slade had figured no one would come looking for him near the Canadian border.

He had lived in an earth lodge, and now that the snows had thawed he planned to follow the Yellowstone River into Montana to a new town called Miles City. Slade hoped to head west from Miles and escape to California, eluding the bounty hunters, crooked lawmen, back-shooters—and especially the long arm of Cliff Langdon, a whip of revenge that shadowed him wherever he went.

Slade had followed the Missouri, past Fort Union, through northern Dakota Territory, taking in the mysterious beauty of the coulees and buttes, both jaggedly lined with strata of sandstone, bentonite clay, shale, and veins of lignite coal.

"Up! Get up! Put your hands over your head!"

Slade threaded his fingers, placed his hands on top of his flattop Stetson, and walked out of the rocks.

A huge, fat man with a star pinned on his black shirt trotted his horse up to Slade. His belly hung over his gun belt like a sack of hay.

"Your name?"

"Who wants to know?"

"Sheriff Bark Taylor. Me and my posse's been lookin' for the man that robbed the bank in Sand Springs."

Slade smiled. "You got the wrong man, Sheriff."

The corner of Taylor's mouth curved in a sneer. "I'll decide that." He worked his leg out of the stirrup and up over the horse, then dismounted.

He puffed and huffed as he walked, the huge bulk of his weight too much for his short, stout frame. "I asked your name, son."

Just in case his reputation had traveled to Montana, Slade said, "Smith . . . Frank Smith."

"Uh huh. Sure. Smith." Taylor ambled closer to Slade and peered into his face. "Check his gear, boys."

Two men worked over the Appaloosa, the heavy packs, a travel bag, a yellow slicker, a bedroll, and the rest of Slade's possibles.

"Holy Jesus!" one of the men exclaimed. "He's got an arsenal here."

The man pulled out Slade's swivel rig. "Shit, looka this! A swivel rig for fast draw, got a slotted plate on the gun belt and a Peacemaker hooked to the plate with a soldered stud. I ain't never seen one of these."

Sheriff Taylor turned and looked. "I heard of 'em."

"A Smith and Wesson pocket thirty-two and a boot pistol. He's got a Winchester rifle layin' over there, and a sawed-off twelve-gauge,'' the man said, pulling the shotgun from the slipper on the horse.

The sheriff moved over to the horse, his fat jiggling. ''Mmm, mmm. He's our man.''

''What the hell are these?'' the other man asked. He held Slade's nitrate caps in his hands, little thimbles of explosive power Slade had had made for him in Rapid City by the same man who fixed up the swivel rig.

Taylor held out his hand. ''Gimme.''

Taylor inspected the nitrate caps. He turned back to Slade. ''What are these?''

''Sinkers for fishin','' Slade lied.

The sheriff handed them back to his deputy, who dropped them back into Slade's travel bag.

A ripple of relief raced through Slade.

''We got him!'' a deputy hollered. ''He's our man for sure.''

Taylor waddled back to Slade's horse.

The deputy lifted Slade's saddlebags from the horse and turned them upside down. Gold coins and greenbacks sprinkled to the ground. The deputy whistled. ''Shit, must be a fortune here.''

Taylor took a look, smiled. His fat face chubbed over his shoulder at Slade. ''How 'bout this? Where'd you get the money?''

''Won it in a poker game back in Deadwood.''

''Sure you did. Probably cleaned out Poker Alice, huh?''

Slade smiled. ''Well, in fact, that's just who I won it from.''

The posse hooted.

''Least he's original, boys. Got a little sense of humor about him.'' Taylor chuckled.

"It's the damn truth," Slade pleaded.

"Tie him up. Let's take him in," Taylor snapped.

A hot twirl of rope cut into Slade's wrists. The posse lifted him to his horse and tied him with underbelly loops to the saddle.

The Appaloosa snorted. Slade put his roped wrists on the saddle horn, tugged the reins, and rode surrounded into the burning sun.

Sand Springs nestled between a ridge of flattop mesas on one side and the Mountain Sheep Bluffs on the other.

The buildings along the dusty street were chipped and worn by the harsh Montana weather. The place looked as though it had seen better days even though it was a young town.

People stopped and watched the posse parade Slade to the sheriff's office. Buckboards pulled over and waited. Taylor led the group triumphantly, proudly.

They pushed Slade into the sheriff's office and led him along a hallway to a thick, wooden door carved into the ground.

"Down there, Smith," Taylor puffed, holding the door open, his fat face bleeding sweat.

"I told you. I'm not your man," Slade said.

"I know, I know. You won all that money from Poker Face Alice back in Deadwood. She always loses."

Taylor dunked Slade into the sod dungeon and slammed the door.

Slade panicked. He tested the dirt walls of the bunker, prowled the small confines. He found a window that sat level with the ground outside. The hole was small, too small for his thin, lean body.

All he could see from the window was the dirt main street, cowboy boots, women's heels.

Slade leapt to the trapdoor, and pounded. It was solid, like stone. He slumped into a corner and sat down.

The stifling heat burned into him. The rope churned on his wrists.

"I can't let fear get the best of me," he mumbled to himself.

He took deep breaths, tried to control his wild mind.

He stayed huddled, hugging his knees until the sun slipped into the ground outside. Sweat rained from his body.

Then the door flew open. "Smith?"

"Yeah?"

"Come up here," Taylor called.

Slade crawled over to the wooden ladder and shimmied up. He emerged from the hole and two deputies grabbed him, yanked him out, pushed him through the hall to the sheriff's office, and slapped him into a chair in front of a desk. Taylor waddled around to the other side and sat down.

"I'm chargin' you with bank robbery, Mr. Smith. You'll stay here in jail until the judge comes and we can convene a jury."

"I told you, I didn't rob your bank."

"You can tell that to the jury, see if they believe you, especially since you're carryin' twenty thousand dollars."

"You can check it out. I won the money in Deadwood."

"And your real name?"

Slade thought about it. If Taylor did check he'd learn the truth about the money. He might also find out Slade was wanted for bank robbery in Kansas. That revelation would go tough on him, but Slade decided to shoot his luck.

"Frank Slade."

"Where you from, Slade?"

"Got no home."

"I see."

"Send a rider, send a wire. I'll pay the expense. Ask Poker Alice. Check with Charlotte Adams there, a woman I knew. I was mining a claim. She holds the title."

"I might check and I might not. Folks here in Sand Springs lost a lot of money in the robbery. Nearly twenty thousand dollars. You'll stay locked up in the hole until we get ready to try you. Take him back, boys."

The two deputies jerked Slade from the chair. He held out his hands. "How 'bout the rope? No need to keep me tied down there."

Taylor smiled. "Okay, cut his hands loose."

One of the deputies cocked a Bowie knife and slit the twisted knot. Slade wiggled his fingers. His wrists were bloody and burned.

The deputies pushed him back down the hall and tossed him into the damp, hot hole.

The days were killing hot, the nights were bone chilling. Slade lost track of time. He lingered in and out of consciousness. His mind replayed the past, flashing back to the day when Cliff Langdon's gang had ridden up to his dad's farm in western Kansas. Over and over again he saw that day in his hallucinating mind . . . how Tripp and his men had killed his mom and dad for the land.

Frank had been hiding in the barn. He was only seventeen but good with a rifle. He'd killed Tripp and his men, then buried his mother and father. He'd dragged the gang into the house and set it on fire, then ridden hard and fast to Texas.

He'd spent years on the southwestern cattle trails and returned to Kansas burning with revenge. He'd found Langdon in his bank and beaten him unmercifully, scarring him for life so the crooked banker would always remember what he'd done, so he'd remember Frank Slade. Slade had taken the money in Langdon's account, but hadn't touched another cent in the bank. Then he'd had Langdon sign a bill of sale for his mom and dad's land.

Slade hadn't wanted to kill the guard outside the bank, but he'd had to, and now he was wanted for robbery and murder in Kansas. He had headed north to Deadwood after the incident in Dodge City, met Boomerang, an old prospector in the Badlands, and together they'd gone to the Black Hills and gotten lucky in mining. Slade had also had a streak with the cards in the Number 10 Saloon and won a big pot from Poker Face Alice.

His best memory of Deadwood was Charlotte Adams, the woman he'd met there and fallen in love with. But Slade had had to leave Deadwood when it became a legal city with lawmen.

Now he was charged with a crime he didn't commit. And there was a good chance they would find out about his past before he came to trial.

If they did, Slade knew he'd hang.

Chapter Two

The door to the bunker opened. Slade shaded his eyes.

"Get up! Come on, get up here!"

Slade had stripped down to his shorts. His body dripped sweat. He was weak with fever, and had no idea how long he'd been in the hole.

He dug his fingers into the curled sod and pulled upright, but fell back to the floor.

"Aw, shit. He's all played out, Hank," one deputy said. "We'll have to pull the bastard out."

"I ain't goin' down in that stinkin' hole, Curly," Hank said. "Jesus, the smell."

"We gotta get him to Taylor's office."

Curly climbed down the steps with a lariat, and gulped and held his breath. He tied the rope around Slade and crawled back up.

They pulled Slade through the opening. He lay weak, wet, reeking, sick.

Taylor lumbered up. "Jesus!" he shouted. "Bucket the bastard down. Clean him off."

Curly went out behind the jail and brought back two pails of water. He splashed them over Slade.

The dousing felt better than anything Slade could remember. His cracked lips tasted the sweetness. He let the deputies drench him, wash him off. Hank threw a blanket over him. Then they dragged Slade to Taylor's office and slammed him into a chair.

Slade was alert now. A chill gripped him as he huddled under the warm blanket.

Taylor smiled. "Like my hospitality?"

Hate slivered through Slade. "Not bad," he said.

"Molly!" Taylor yelled. "How 'bout a cup of coffee, some biscuits and gravy for our guest?"

Taylor's wife walked in from the living quarters next to the office. She stood behind Slade, but he heard her voice.

"It'll be a few minutes."

"That's okay, Mr. Slade will wait. Right, Slade?"

Slade nodded.

Taylor produced a bottle of whiskey from his desk, poured a barrel glass half full, and handed it to Slade. "Here, have a drink. Should help that fever."

Slade sipped slowly. The raw whiskey hit his empty belly like a flaming arrow.

"Good, huh?" Taylor asked.

"It'll do," Slade said, more alert and awake.

"We got some business to talk about, Slade," the sheriff said.

Molly Taylor walked in and set a plate of biscuits and

gravy on the edge of the desk. Slade took the fork, and his hand shook as he dug in. He knew he had to eat slowly or he'd retch it all back up.

Slade sipped the whiskey, took another bite, and looked up at the woman who stood beside the desk. She had long brown hair, a beautiful square-cut face, thick lips, and steamy brown eyes. Her dress hugged her waist and was low cut with frilly lace on her chest.

Slade looked back over at Taylor. He had to be fifteen years older than the woman, and because he looked to be around forty-five, Molly would be near thirty. It didn't make sense to Slade that a beautiful woman like Molly would be married to a slob like Taylor.

''Where's my money?'' Slade asked.

''Locked in that safe over there. Evidence for the trial.''

''I didn't rob the bank.''

''Oh, I know that now, Slade.''

Slade almost dropped his fork. Molly offered him coffee. He held the warm cup in his hands and brought it to his lips. ''If you know that, why are you holding me?''

''The money taken from the bank was all new greenbacks. That money you got is old.''

''You'll let me go now,'' Slade said, a shimmer of hope rippling through his recuperating body.

''Not that easy,'' Taylor said.

''What's the problem?''

''I'll have to do some checking on you, Slade. See where you got all that money.''

''I told you, I won it in a poker game.''

''I don't believe that, but there's a new marshal down in Deadwood. We'll find out, won't we?''

"And if I'm telling the truth?"

Taylor leaned back. "I can tell a man that's on the run. I think I'll find out more than a poker story about you, Slade."

Slade ate slowly, slurping the coffee, relishing every second of freedom from the dirty hole.

"So, you'll be stayin' as my guest a few more days until I get the full story on you."

"What would you say if I split that money with you? Would you let me go?" Slade offered.

Taylor chuckled. "Why should I take half when one way or another I'm gonna get it all?"

Chapter Three

Slade sat in the corner of the hole. He tried to sort things out. Taylor would learn Slade won the money in a poker game at the Number 10 Saloon in Deadwood, but he'd also hear about the gunfight with the Pueblo Kid and the warrant for Slade's arrest in Kansas.

"Shit," Slade mumbled. "He'll come back, steal all my money, then pick up the reward for my capture." The idea of a redneck crook like Taylor stealing his poker winnings, then collecting the reward on top of that, made Slade shudder with hate.

But what could he do? There was no way he could dig out of the dirt jail, and if he had to spend several more days locked in the heat of the days and the chill of the nights, he'd be a dead man.

Slade fell asleep thinking about a good steak, a fine

woman, and freedom. He cuddled under the blanket in a fetal position in the corner of the bunker.

He awakened and sat with his back straight against the wall. He tried to hypnotize himself into health, using the technique of mind control he'd learned from the Pueblo Kid when they were friends riding together in Texas.

Slade heard a rustling, a scraping above, then the door to the hole opened.

"He's gone, hurry," Molly Taylor said.

Slade wrapped the blanket around his shivering body and pulled himself up the ladder and through the opening.

"God, you're a mess," Molly whispered. "Can you walk?"

"I can make it," Slade mumbled, a light of hope igniting his weak body. He followed Molly through the dark hall to Taylor's office, then into the living quarters.

Molly pointed to a bedroom. "I've filled the tub. Take a bath and I'll fix you a meal."

"You wouldn't have a good steak, maybe a T-bone?" Slade asked.

"No, but I can fix fresh elk."

Slade's mouth salivated. "Sounds good," he murmured.

He went to the adjoining room and climbed into an oak tub Molly had filled with hot water. The warmth of the bath caressed his tired body and gave Slade a new strength.

But what the hell was going on? Why was Molly Taylor doing this? Slade tried to plan a getaway. He'd seen no deputies. Although he had no way of knowing, he figured it was the middle of the night.

He stepped out of the tub and dried himself with a towel Molly had left. He tied it around his waist, then walked into the living room.

Molly stood at the stove. "Feel better?"

"A little like a human being again," Slade said. "I was stinkin' so bad I couldn't stand myself."

"I've got some fresh clothes in the other room for you, but you look comfortable and glowing. I'll get them later. Sit down."

Slade took a chair at the kitchen table.

Molly smiled. "A good meal and you'll feel like a new man."

"And the sheriff?" Slade asked.

She served him a cup of steaming coffee. "He rode up to James City to check on you. He said he'd send a wire to Deadwood and wait for the news."

Slade cupped the coffee in his hands and sipped.

"And what will Bark find in Deadwood, Mr. Slade?" Molly asked, turning from the stove, wiping her hands on a blue apron that was tied tightly around her waist.

Slade looked up, gazed at the woman's beauty, her slim waist bodiced snugly, her pearlike breasts, the long sweep of her pink calico dress.

She walked to the table and slid a plate full of potatoes smothered with lard and a thick elk steak in front of Slade.

"You can tell me, Mr. Slade. I think we have a lot in common."

"I didn't rob the bank here," Slade said.

"I know that, Bark knows that, and you know that. Doesn't make any difference. He's going to take your money one way or the other."

"I figured that much," Slade said, chewing on a piece of meat, scooping up some hot spuds.

"And if you're on the run, like Bark thinks, if you have a past, it'll go hard on you."

"This is a good steak, ma'am."

Molly sat down across from Slade. She leaned her smooth cheek on her hand. "Why don't you tell me?" she said softly.

"Why don't *you* tell me?"

"Why I let you out?"

"Yes, that and why you've cooked me this meal."

"I have my reasons."

Slade smiled. "No doubt about that, ma'am."

"I thought you might help me get out of this rotten town," Molly said.

Slade took another bite of elk, chewed it slowly, ate some potatoes, then sipped coffee. Finally, he said, "Good-lookin' woman like you, seems you could find a man to take you out of Sand Springs easy enough."

"Could be," Molly said, "but no man ever came through here before who had twenty thousand dollars."

Slade finished his steak and leaned back, his coffee cup in one hand. "Just what *are* you doing in this town, Mrs. Taylor?"

"Long story. No time to tell it."

"I thought so. And what are you doing with a man like Bark Taylor? Is that another long story?"

"I'm afraid so."

"I see," Slade said, understanding her reticence.

"Let's say I'm here 'cause I can't leave," Molly whispered.

"The sheriff? He's got something on you maybe?"

"That's the only reason, Mr. Slade. I've been here two years. If I threatened to leave I'd be in trouble."

"Which means you were in trouble before you got here, right? Before you came to Sand Springs?"

Molly got up and went to the stove. "You want some more potatoes?"

"I'm full up now," Slade said. "Tell me about it. Tell my why you're here, why you let me out, and how much of my twenty thousand dollars you want."

Molly turned from the big, black stove. She smiled. "The money's still in the safe."

"And you know the combination, right?"

"I might," she said, walking to the table and standing over Slade, her hands on her waist, her hips rolling under the calico.

Slade had liked the Northern Dakota Indians. They had welcomed him, made him feel at home as he hid out the winter from the law and Cliff Langdon. But it had been a long time since he'd seen a good-looking white woman.

He reached up, yanked Molly onto his lap, and gave her a good, hard kiss. She pressed her bodice, the soft swirls of her big boobs, against his naked chest, then moved suggestively on his legs.

"Wanna make a deal?" she asked, her voice husky and low.

"Do I have a choice?" Slade asked.

Molly stood up. The towel around Slade's belly ripped away. His cock shimmied and thumped upward. He pushed his chair back from the table.

Molly's eyes gazed at Slade's lean, muscular body, his thin but sinewy frame, his jaggedly handsome face, the slick, wet black hair.

Slade wondered if her deal was simply to let him out of the hole, use him, then have him slammed back into the bunker.

Molly reached down and fisted Slade's hardness. "Damn!" she huffed.

"I been with the Indians for the winter," Slade explained lamely.

Molly's hand inspected Slade's stiff cock. "Holy sweetness!"

Slade lifted her dress. Molly was naked underneath. Her flat belly, the lush lines of her hips, the glowing brown triangle between her legs made Slade shudder with excitement.

She straddled Slade and screwed down.

"Ooof!" she whispered.

Slade was in. He placed his hands on her thin waist. Molly swung her arms around his neck.

"Good, that feels good, Slade," Molly said.

Slade figured he had an edge on her now. "I like it too, Miz Taylor, but I'd like it a lot more if I knew I was gonna walk out of this stinking place in a few minutes."

"You will, you will. I promise. But not before you pleasure me."

Slade pumped off the chair.

"Ahhfff!" Molly shrieked.

She became a wild animal on top of Slade, bouncing up and down, her plump rear slapping on his thighs. She bucked and held on with her hands around his neck. Slade pushed, spiking up from the chair.

Molly's mouth was unhinged. She looked down into Slade's face. Their eyes met. Then they made it.

"Now, Slade!" Molly yelled. "Now!"

She jerked, bounced, then shook furiously. Slade let her take him, let the flow of his repressed winter passion flood into her like a warm spring thaw.

Chapter Four

Molly walked to the cupboard and pulled down a bottle of Sheriff Taylor's whiskey, a cheap trade bourbon Taylor had no doubt received as a gift from the local saloon operator.

"Drink?"

"You bet," Slade said.

Molly poured two glasses half full and set one in front of Slade, then slid into a chair across from him at the kitchen table.

"It's like this," she said. "I know where Bark has hidden the combination to the safe. I'll tell you if you'll split the twenty thousand with me."

"Ouch!" Slade said.

"You offered Bark half for your freedom," she said.

"I guess I did," Slade admitted.

Molly's smile faded. "I hate to sound cold, but that's the deal. You can walk out of here a free man right now.

I might come under suspicion for letting you go, but I can talk my way out of it.'' Molly hesitated, lifted her glass to her soft, thick lips, took a gentle sip, and continued. "But you'd leave without your money."

"And if I split with you?"

"You get half, and I go with you."

"Where?"

"I don't expect to stay with you, get that straight, but I'd like to find a place and catch a train out to California. I don't ever wanna see Montana again."

"I see," Slade said.

Molly followed up quickly. "And if you're thinkin' of makin' me a deal, then taking the money back later, I wouldn't if I were you."

Slade sipped his whiskey. He had to accept Molly's offer. He needed the combination. He wanted out of Sand Springs as badly as she did.

"I'm a man of my word," Slade said. "That's all I got. I seen men cheat before. That's why I'm on the run, I wouldn't abide by it. My freedom, gettin' out of this hole, out of Sand Springs, is worth ten grand to me."

Molly extended her hand across the table. "You help me get through to Yellowstone City, south of here along the river. The Sioux find me alone and you know what would happen. You know what they'd do to a white woman like me. There's a new stage line in Yellowstone City. I can take it down toward Wyoming or Deadwood in Dakota."

Slade shook her hand and said, "Deal."

They sat for a few moments sizing each other up, then Slade asked, "When did your husband leave? How much head start do we have?"

"He should be in James City by tomorrow. He'll have

to wait a day or so for an answer from Deadwood, another day and a half to get back here to Sand Springs . . . gives us about a three-day advantage.''

Slade saw the look of doubt on her face. ''Except what?'' he asked.

''The deputies will find out I'm gone. They'll find out we're both gone.''

''When will they check the hole?''

''Usually at dawn. But with Bark gone, they'll be late. They always are when he's out of town.''

''So, if we leave now we'll have maybe a nine- or ten-hour lead on them?''

''But they'll organize a posse,'' Molly warned.

''When?''

''Most likely they'll wait for Bark to get back, but I can't say for sure. At any rate, we got a head start if you wanna get going.''

''Then let's move. The combination?'' Slade asked.

''Your clothes first,'' she said, leading Slade to the bedroom. She handed him a new pair of Levi's, a blue chambray shirt, a Levi's jacket, and a fresh pair of balbriggans. Slade dressed as Molly watched.

''My husband's a mean man, Slade. He'll be enraged about this, the two of us together. He'll hunt us both, especially you.''

Slade thought about the warrant out for his arrest back in Kansas, about the lawmen and gunmen probably on his trail even as they talked. He shrugged.

Molly led Slade to Taylor's office. She opened a drawer at the bottom of the sheriff's desk and pulled out a sheet of paper. ''Here,'' she said.

Slade knelt in front of the safe. He turned the knob and listened to the tumblers. They clicked like a pick shattering a block of ice. The door popped open. He pulled out his saddlebags and handed them to Molly.

Slade went to the gun rack on the far wall. He lifted his Winchester, then opened the cabinet and took out his possibles, his swivel rig, nitrate caps, and his other weapons.

Molly counted out her ten grand and gave the saddlebags back to Slade. She disappeared, and returned in riding clothes.

"Are you ready?"

"Horses?" Slade asked.

"Out back."

"My Appaloosa?"

"No, I would have had to go to the livery. They would have talked. There's always some horses out in back. We just need to saddle up. There's a couple of good roans."

She looked good in her buckskin jacket and pants, and her riding boots. "I'll put some food up for the trip," she said.

"Just some flour and fatback, so we can travel light. We'll shoot some prairie chickens, a rabbit, maybe a squirrel."

"Whiskey?" Molly smirked.

"I'll have to admit I was about to ask," Slade said.

They slipped out the back door. Slade saddled and cinched the horses. He tied their gear on, and they rode slowly through the back alleys of Sand Springs, then down a narrow trail that led out into the dark Montana night.

Slade took a deep breath. He'd escaped another noose. If he'd believed in God, he might have offered up a prayer of thanks. But Slade was a doubter. He relied on the law

of cause and effect . . . that was his god. An impersonal
god. He knew the law worked no matter how you used
it. Good or bad.

Through the same dark night Jubal Holiday galloped
out of the Black Hills, leaning his weight into the stirrups of his orange-brown sorrel.

Jubal was tired, worn out. Hunting men was tough
business, but Frank Slade would be his biggest score. If
he took Slade it would make all the territorial papers
and lend credibility to his legend.

Since early boyhood Jubal had wanted to make a name
in the West. Now, at thirty-seven, he'd had more gun-
fights than he could remember, and he'd won them all.

Jubal's trip to Deadwood had been disappointing. He'd
hoped for more leads, but Wild Bill was dead, Calamity
Jane had refused to discuss Slade, and Poker Alice had
left for Cheyenne on a shopping trip.

Holiday had counted on a break from the woman
named Charlotte Adams, the lady Slade had taken up
with in Deadwood, but she had died in the Deadwood
fire.

He had checked the recorder's office and found the
mining claim Slade had worked. The mine was in Charlotte's name. When it went up for sale with the other
mines unclaimed after the fire, Holiday had purchased
the claim for Cliff Langdon.

Jubal's body ached for Frank Slade. Slade had robbed
a bank, mutilated the owner, killed the guard. Sure,
there was Slade's side of the story, but Holiday had
enough experience to know that every outlaw in the West
would try to justify his actions, just as Slade had been
trying to do.

Jubal had heard word around Deadwood that Slade had headed for Denver. Holiday figured that news to be a diversion. Denver was too close to Kansas, where Slade was wanted. No, he figured if Slade had been attracted to the gold strikes in the Black Hills, then he'd be drawn to the new bonanza over in Montana.

Just a hunch, but a man like Holiday worked hunches. That was how he made his living. A good living. Fine hotel rooms, excellent whiskey, pretty women.

He'd had the best.

Holiday didn't know much regarding Frank Slade, but he'd learned enough about Slade's life in Deadwood to give him cause for concern—especially the way Slade had gunned down the Pueblo Kid. The Kid had been one of the fastest draws working the West.

But Holiday liked a good challenge. He'd find Frank Slade and take him because losing was repugnant to Holiday.

He dug the spokes of his spurs into the flank of his horse and headed across the border into Montana Territory.

Chapter Five

Slade and Molly rode hard down the Yellowstone River toward Yellowstone City. The sun came up and an early heat seared the rugged landscape.

They reached a crook in the river at sundown and pulled up. Slade slipped out of his saddle and helped Molly down.

"God. I'm stiff. I haven't done any riding like that," she said.

"Fix a campfire, set things out. I'll hunt up a couple of prairie chickens for supper," he said.

Slade unhitched his saddle, put it on the ground, and laid out his gun rigs. He kept his saddlebags with his half of the money. Slade was rusty after a calm winter with the Indians. He hadn't decided about Molly. He had to be careful. He took his rifle and walked off into the thick brush near the river.

Prairie chickens were as plentiful as buffalo. It didn't

take Slade long to nail two plump birds. He hung them by the neck from his belt and walked back to camp.

Molly had built a fire near a circle of boulders at the edge of the river, right next to a bluff. A good place out of the wind. She smiled as Slade walked into the camp.

"You got a couple," she said.

"Nice fat hens," Slade returned. "I'll pluck 'em."

He sat down and jerked the feathers from the birds, then split them with his Eagle knife. He handed the hens to Molly. She rolled them in flour and fried them in melting fatback. A blue enamel coffeepot boiled over the crackling flames of the fire.

They sat around the glow as the night descended. A blue-black sky hung over them. The air turned cold. The fire felt good. The birds were crisp, tasty. They pulled the parts and feasted on the wild meat.

"God, I'm excited about getting out of this country," Molly said.

"You'll make it."

"What about you, Slade?"

Slade was new on the run, but he'd learned one thing during his flight from prosecution—never tell anyone your real plans. "Don't exactly know," he said.

They finished eating and sat in the orange shadows that leapt from the campfire. The evening turned chilly. Slade moved their saddles together against the rock. Molly rolled out two blankets and spread them on the ground. Slade loosened his roll and handed her his Indian blanket.

Molly lay down, her head on her saddle. Slade poured the coffee over the lingering coals of the fire, then joined her. Molly snuggled close. "I suppose you think bad of me."

"Naw."

"Takin' your money and all. Our bargain?"

"We made a deal. I'll stick by it."

Molly pressed closer. Slade slid an arm around her and hugged tighter. She felt good. Her hips rolled slowly. Slade's hard cock punched into her buckskin pants.

Her fingers tapped between them, snaked over Slade's belly, and rubbed into the bulge in his Levi's. Slade's hand slid down her back, fluttered into the soft luxury of her ass.

Molly threw the Indian blanket off, stood up, and took her clothes off. The cluster of stars and the bright moon outlined her beauty, her fine body. She knelt beside Slade, unhooked his pants, and pulled them down over his slim hips, his long, sinewy legs.

Molly bent over. Her lips brushed the tip of Slade's hard offering. He stiffened.

His fingers threaded her soft hair. Molly dipped up and down. Slade thought he'd never be able to hang back, hold down the raging that seethed within him.

Molly rolled over, straddled him, hooked her legs on either side of him. She sat up on her knees and clutched Slade's hardness, manipulated it gently along her thighs, then pushed him in.

She rocked slowly on top of Slade, bending his erection back and forth, making love to him. She worked slowly at first, then furiously, slamming up and down at him, consuming him.

Slade put his feet flat on the blanket, lifted up, and spiked her with short, quick jabs.

"Yeah!" Molly squealed. "Fuck me!"

She shuddered and fell on top of him. Her hot breath,

the huffing and puffing, tickled Slade's ear. Her hair dangled in his face. He lifted her and she rolled over, then snuggled beside him. He found the Indian blanket and covered Molly. He slipped under the blanket and crawled into the warmth and security of Molly's open legs. She hooked him in.

''Too bad we can't just stay here like this,'' she whispered, her fingers scratching lightly on his back.

Slade smiled cynically. Isn't that what Charlotte Adams had said to him in Deadwood? Didn't he know by now he'd never stay in one place very long, never settle down, never have a woman or a home?

Slade was on the run again, but as he lay under the stars, in the cradle of Molly's legs, he knew he'd done the right thing back in Kansas. Fortuna's wheel spins a wicked twist. Slade was still young, still learning, but he made a silent oath. Wherever there was a crooked lawman, a corrupt businessman, a deceitful lawyer, a cheater and a liar, he'd be on the other side . . . and in the West he lived in that would be often. Slade didn't mind. He figured it would be like this for him in any other century.

But what if he'd been born into the Hearst family? He'd probably be in a fine school in the East. He'd be rich. His pa would own the Homestake Gold Mine Company in Deadwood.

The dice had already clicked. Fortuna's wheel had taken a spin and Slade had come up on the run.

Molly's hand feathered between them. Slade lifted, and she put him in. It would be easy to take his money back and leave her, but she'd hook back up with Taylor, and then he'd have a kidnapping hanging over him in addition to the sheriff's phony charges.

It had been a long time. Slade liked the feel of being with a woman again. The cold winter, the long months hiding out in an earth hut, tramping through snow knee-high to hunt game had left Slade in need of a woman's softness, a woman's warmth.

He rocked up and down. What would life be like without women? Slade wondered, as Molly crossed her legs behind him and tugged him deeper.

Women were the only fine thing in the West. Maybe women could tame it. Maybe women could change the killing, stealing, lying, cheating.

Molly bucked under him.

Slade thumped faster.

"I love this!" Molly shouted. "I love screwin' like this!"

"It's a good thing," Slade whispered. "It's about the only good thing in life."

An owl hooted. Molly gulped in a choking breath, then shook uncontrollably. Her legs tightened around Slade, her hips banged up at him.

Slade's strokes were long, smooth, and sure. He felt her fingernails clip into his shoulders. She wound her arms around his neck, pulled him down, and kissed him.

A ripple slid through Slade's lean body. He released all his confusion as he rocked hard, then slumped down into Molly's warmth and fell asleep.

Chapter Six

S lade hadn't tested his built-in alarm system in a long time. He could usually hypnotize his mind to be alert even though he was asleep, keep tuned to danger around him, but the long winter months, the draining of his passion and energy had left him weak and spent.

Dream pictures flipped through his mind . . . Charlotte Adams in Deadwood, the money he'd left with her to deposit in the Deadwood bank, his mining claim. He dreamed about the long ride to escape Deadwood, up to the Missouri River in the northeast corner of the territory, living with the peaceful Mandan Indians.

Slade dreamed about the gray, cold days in a sod igloo built of cottonwood posts, sapling beams, willow branches, and prairie grass.

He dreamed of howling blizzards, the endless cold, the slate-dark skies, eating greasy, rubbery buffalo; but most of all he dreamed of Cliff Langdon back down in Kansas, how Langdon had devoted part of his life to finding and killing Slade.

When Slade awoke, Molly was gone.

He hadn't learned yet. He hadn't been on the run long enough. He'd miscalculated his odds. He had to understand . . . *you don't trust anyone.*

He leapt up. His horse was gone and so was his money. Slade stalked the camp, his boots digging into the soft earth around the river bank. He found a sack of gold near the dead campfire. He sat down and counted out five hundred dollars.

"Generous bitch," he mumbled.

Slade sat back and sorted out his options. Molly was obviously on her way to Deadwood. Smart woman. There was no way Slade could follow, not after his shoot-out there with the Pueblo Kid, not with a deputy marshal in town, a lawman who by now would know everything about Frank Slade.

He got up and walked to the river's edge, found a boulder, and sat in the bright morning sun. He took a deep breath, held it, then exhaled slowly and lifted his face to the sun. Soon a posse would be on the way from Sand Springs with Taylor riding lead.

Slade needed to think, calm down, figure things out. He sat meditating on his situation for several minutes before a thought hit him.

A raft!

He could build a raft and sail it down to Miles City. Time was against him. But he could pull it off. It was a good idea. Taylor and his posse would never figure it.

Slade went to work immediately. He found two trees snapped at the trunk. He hacked them apart with his hatchet, split them open, and laid four logs together that made a raft about three feet wide and five feet long.

He hoisted the logs to his shoulder and started back toward the river. His leg jammed down into a traphole. His ankle twisted. The logs sailed forward and Slade sprawled to the ground.

He wrenched his boot out of the hole, but he'd hurt his ankle badly. Pain shot through his right leg. Slade stood up. He had a serious sprain. He tried the ankle. Hot pain. He fell back to the ground, struggled back to his pack, and pulled out a lariat. He tossed the rope in the water and soaked it, then tied the logs together with strong knots.

Pain screamed through his foot, up into his leg. Slade slugged down three gulps of whiskey from the bottle of bourbon Molly had packed, then crawled to a birch tree, hacked it down, cut it again, and carved a crude paddle with his Eagle knife.

Slade got up, limped with the paddle back to the river's edge, to the newly made raft, and gathered together his possibles for the trip. He pulled down another shot of whiskey to dull the searing pain. He limped, falling now and then, around the campsite, brushing his tracks away with the bristles of a bantra bush. He buried the fire, swept over his tracks backward to the river, loaded up, and pushed off.

The current sent him downstream. Slade paddled alongside the raft, nosing it forward. The sun hit noon. He lay on his back and let the raft drift while he dangled his injured foot in the cold water of the Yellowstone.

Slade was surprised how fast the river floated him south. He worked with the craft into the afternoon, steering forward until dusk, paddling hard through the night.

The morning sun stretched over the cottonwoods along the bank of the Yellowstone. Slade rounded a bend in the river and saw a cluster of buildings on the prairie ahead. He was on his knees, his bad foot curled behind him. He paddled his birch branch and moved the craft close to shore along the Fort Keogh Cantonment. Slade could see why they had built the Cantonment near the confluence of the Yellowstone and Tongue Rivers.

A sound military decision. The thick timber along the Tongue offered protection from blasting winter storms and provided a generous source of fuel and building material.

The big cottonwoods had bark torn from the upper side of the trunks near the ground. An ice gorge had obviously floated through the area in the past . . . and would again.

But Slade had more important things on his mind than the geographical location of Fort Keogh and its companion settlement, Miles City.

He landed the raft on a muddy bank near town, and stood up. His ankle felt better. He gathered his pack, bedroll, slicker, and saddlebags, then pushed the raft back into the river and let it sail listlessly away.

Slade limped along the bank of the Yellowstone into Miles City. The Carlson House sat on the edge of Main Street near the river.

Slade's foot still hurt. He limped up the steps and walked into the warm lobby. An old man with a gray beard got up from a chair behind the counter where he was reading the Yellowstone *Journal*.

"Came in across the river, huh?" he said appraising Slade with strong, blue eyes.

Slade looked down at his wet Levi's. "Can I get some dry clothes?"

"Right down Main Street." The old man chuckled. "That's what we call our main street, *Main Street*."

Slade had to struggle to be civil. He smiled.

"Yeah, and we got all the necessities to support life in this part of the country. We're a growin' cattle town, a lusty man's town. We got legal gambling, alcohol, dance houses, parlor houses, anything you want. Even got a tailor who does repairs. It's a trooper's town mostly. You probably saw the army down along the cantonment."

"I did," said Slade.

"In fact, for a man who looks like he's been travelin' hard like you, I could send a bottle of good liquor along with a woman to your room."

"I'll take the bottle and pass on the woman." Slade smiled, realizing what the old man was about.

A short, nattily dressed man walked in from a side door. His ruddy cheeks, round face, and dignified presence gave him a rich look.

"Jedediah always offers our male customers liquor and women, sir. It's our policy, and we have a legal license for both."

Slade ignored the man and found a five-dollar gold piece in his pocket. He plunked it on the counter. "You say mostly troops in town?"

Jedediah smiled. "Bunch of hellions, but they make things interesting around here. Sure you don't want a woman?"

"Just some dry clothes. I'll walk down to the store

and buy some, then I'll come back and we'll look at your rooms. I have some inclinations about what I want, where it should be.''

"You have chosen the finest hotel west of Deadwood, sir," the well-dressed man said. "I'm Angus Carlson, your host. Give the man his change for that gold piece, Jedediah."

Slade shook his hand.

"I understand about your room," Carlson said. "Don't want to be on the first floor, right? Too dangerous?"

Slade nodded.

"Take good care of our guest, Jedediah, and if I can be of personal service to you during your stay, sir, call on me," Carlson said. He smiled and walked back toward the door through which he had emerged earlier as if on cue.

"I'll get you a bottle, heat up some water for your room," Jedediah said. "Didn't get your name?"

"Didn't give it."

"You have to sign in. You got to register."

Slade grabbed the thick book and scrawled an X. No way he'd sign in under his real name.

"An X?" the old clerk said. "Just like our sheriff. He always signs with an X."

"Would that be X. Biedler?" Slade asked. He'd heard about Biedler and his reputation as an honest lawman, a fast gun with iron courage.

"Hank Wormwood is the sheriff, but Biedler works with him."

"Thanks for the information," Slade said.

Jedediah smiled again. His teeth were stained brown

from chew. "Thought you might wanna know that. Bet you can write your name too, huh?"

"Let's say I can, and let's say it's Frank Slade, and let's say if anyone comes asking for me that I'm not here, okay?" Slade said, then rolled another gold coin across the counter at the old man.

"Mr. Carlson's real particular about protecting the confidentiality of our guests, Mr. Slade. You can depend on us. No, sir, never heard of Frank Slade." The old man chuckled, pocketing the gold coin. "But I'll bet if I was to ask around I'd find he's the one who killed a bunch of men down in Deadwood."

Slade was tiring of the old man's banter. "But if you talked to Frank Slade personally, he'd say he's never been in Deadwood."

"I get your drift," Jedediah said. "I'll fetch you some whiskey and warm water. You'll find the Hubbell store just down the street. You can get some new clothes there."

Chapter Seven

Miles City was born as Milestown in 1876. Slade knew the history. He'd heard about Miles City, how General Miles had tired of all the coffee-coolers hanging on at the Tongue River cantonment. Slade disliked the coolers, cowardly men and women who always camped near the army troops for protection.

General Miles had ordered all the coolers out of camp. They'd set up tents on the other side of the Tongue River and built saloons, a gambling hall, log huts, and log cabins.

Miles City was a tough town, and Slade felt good dragging his limp ankle from one patch of boardwalk to the other, his gear over his shoulder. He knew this was a town with characters, soldiers, whores, and twenty-four-hour entertainment.

A Diamond R bull train pulled through Main Street.

Slade had seen the trademark everywhere on the trails of the West. Diamond R had offices in New York City, Boston, Philadelphia, Chicago, St. Louis, and St. Paul.

Three Diamond R wagons were loaded to the top, pulled by twelve yoke of bulls. A bull-whacker walked proudly back by the wheelers, lashing out with his whip. The popper chewed into the bulls' hides, took a bite of hair.

Main Street had been crowded with troopers, cowboys, buckboards, jerkies—wagons controlled by jerkline string between driver and animal—but they all pulled over and made room for the bull train.

Students from the military institute at Fort Keogh jeered and made fun of the train and its crew.

"Bunch of sogers," Slade mumbled.

Off to his right men worked putting down track for the new Northern Pacific, which was extending its line from Bismarck in Dakota Territory over to Billings. The town smelled like money, which pleased Slade because he was broke again.

Slade passed Charlie Brown's Saloon, John Chinnick's Saloon, The Grand Central Hotel, Miles and Stevell's Hardware Store, the Keg Saloon, C. W. Savage and Company, the steamboat building, and the Yellowstone *Journal*. He finally came to Hubbell's General Merchandise.

"I need to outfit," Slade told the clerk. "Black pants, white shirt with ruffles, a new bandanna, black coat."

"No problem," the man said.

"Pretty high prices," Slade observed.

"Nothin' in this store or in Miles City under two bits, mister."

Slade took the new outfit and walked out onto Main, down past Bill Reece's Dance Hall, the First National Bank, the Cottage Saloon, Professor Bach's Restaurant, the Park Hotel, Kitty Hardiman's Dance Hall, making his way finally to Jordan's tailor shop. He had his clothes fitted so they hugged his body. Slade didn't like baggy clothes. They made him feel sloppy, uncomfortable. Bad for a fast draw.

"Can you have these done by this afternoon and deliver them to me at the Carlson House?" he asked.

"Sure, but that'll be an extra dollar."

Slade paid up and went back to the hotel. Jedediah was sitting behind the check-in counter reading the paper. He jumped up.

"Got you a good bottle of whiskey, and you got hot water waitin' for you." The old man smiled.

"Let's look at some rooms."

Jedediah led him to the second floor and showed him a room in the back. Slade checked the window. He peered down into an alley below. He tried the bed and said, "This'll do."

"Thought so," the clerk said, showing him his tobacco-stained smile. "I thought you'd like the privacy, and you got a good look down to the alley."

"I have some clothes coming over from the tailor. You'll let me know when they get here?"

Jedediah set the bottle of whiskey on the chiffonier and said, "Sure. And I'll go get your hot water. A pail for you to wash up and one for that bad foot."

Slade sat down, pulled off his boot, and soaked his swollen ankle in a pail of steaming water. He sighed and leaned back on his elbows. The bed felt good. He submerged his foot until the water turned lukewarm, then he poured the tin basin on the chiffonier full with fresh water and scrubbed down.

He pulled on a fresh pair of balbriggans and lay back on the soft, welcome bed, his Colt by his side, his Winchester against the wall near the head of the bed.

Slade twisted the cork on the whiskey, fisted the neck, and took a long swallow. It burned down his chest and splashed into his empty stomach like a hot rope.

He propped the bottle between his legs and relaxed, listening to the howl and whoop of the troopers, the tinkling pianos, the creak of buckboards on the street below.

Slade pulled down another swig of whiskey. He felt better now. Ready. Alert. His ankle had stopped paining. He check his Colt, tested the hammer tension. He loaded the rifle, and silently thanked the Winchester Company for recently making their rifles compatible with a Colt .45 slug. Meant less ammunition he had to haul around.

He took another drink, put the bottle on the stand beside the bed, and lay back, his .45 in his hand, the Winchester resting by his side.

One day he'd make enough money and take a river-boat to Missouri, down to St. Louis. Then maybe he'd connect to a big steamer headed for New Orleans, go south, and disappear.

But until he could afford that kind of luxury, Slade had to be ready. He was angry, his body fluid. He knew what would happen. If he could make his bum ankle work, he'd trick them.

Slade put on his old jeans. They were still wet, and clung to his lower body. He went to the window and pushed it higher, as far as he could get it open, then crawled out onto the ledge circling the hotel under his room. He had his Colt with him. He worked his way to the next room. The window was open and he peeked in. Empty. He wiggled through the window, set his .45 on the bed, and crawled back to his own room. He grabbed his rifle and edged back along the ledge to the next room.

He slipped through the window opening, went in, and lay back on the bed with his weapons. Two hours later he heard the scratching of boots on the stairs. He sat up, back straight. He clicked the Colt, laid it on the bed, picked up the rifle, and levered a shell into the chamber.

The door slammed open in the next room, his room.

Gunfire.

Slade slipped along the wall, pulled the door open, and crept into the hall.

"Shit, he ain't here," he heard Sheriff Taylor say.

Slade knelt against the wall. He leveled the Winchester in front of him. Two deputies emerged from his room. He waited until they were all out, waited until Taylor, huffing and puffing under the bulk of his fat, came into the hallway.

"I reckon you gentlemen would be lookin' for me," Slade drawled.

They wheeled around.

Slade pumped the Winchester.

Taylor and his men were caught. The deputies went down. Slade rolled across the hall to avoid shots from Taylor's gun, then sprang back up on one knee.

"Drop it!" he whispered.

Taylor's gun arm went limp. His Navy Special dropped to the floor. "You killed my men," he said. "You killed 'em both."

"What a shame," Slade said, rising. "And you're lucky to be alive, you fat worm."

"I resent that!" Taylor hissed.

Slade smiled. "You're under the gun and you're offended about your weight. Vanity in the face of death. You amaze me."

"Where's Molly?" Taylor asked.

"How would I know?"

Taylor trembled with rage. "She left with you, right?"

"I lost her trail after she stole my money. Guess we got one thing in common, Sheriff. She took us both."

"Don't lie!" Taylor shouted.

Slade levered a new shell into the Winchester.

"Now, hold it. Wait a minute here, Slade. We can make a deal."

"I'd like to make you a deal like you made me back in Sand Springs. Nice dark hole. Steal my money."

"That was just a misunderstanding."

"A crooked sheriff doing business, right?" Slade said sarcastically.

"You got me wrong, Slade."

Slade moved closer, rifle ready.

"This'll go against you in the long run, Slade, so don't be rash here."

Slade laughed. He jammed the butt of the rifle into Taylor's jaw. Taylor spun and bounced off the hall wall. He went for his gun. Slade caught him and punched the stalk of his Winchester into Taylor's belly.

"Look, let me talk to you," Taylor pleaded, falling to his knees.

"Shut up!"

"Please, now, listen to me . . ."

"I hate crooked lawmen, Taylor."

Taylor reached for a vest gun. Slade shot him. It was neat. A hole between the eyes. Blood streamed down onto Taylor's nose. He slumped into the wall, then slithered to death in a big, fat ball.

Jedediah, his boots clapping, came puffing up the stairs.

Slade turned the rifle on him.

"They made me. They made me tell 'em you were up here."

Slade let the rifle go loose in his hand.

"They threatened to kill me, Mr. Slade."

"Get some help. Take these bodies down by the river and bury them. Then come back here and keep your mouth shut. You understand?" Slade growled.

"That's what I'm gonna do," said Jedediah.

Angus Carlson rounded the hall. "Indeed you will, Jedediah. You'll do exactly as Mr. Slade says. Bury these men down by the river, and if you so much as let one word slip you'll be fired."

"Thanks," Slade said. "I'll recommend you in my travels."

Slade walked into his original room. Carlson followed him. "We'll keep this quiet, Mr. Slade. I see no reason to tell anyone about it, and from what I overheard it sounded like you got a bum deal up there in Sand Springs."

"I didn't rob their bank if that's what you're gettin' at," Slade said. "I made the money legal in Deadwood.

Taylor was going to steal all of it from me, but his wife beat him to it.''

"I see," Carlson said. "I see. How long will you be in Miles City, Slade?"

"Long enough to enjoy some leisure. I've had a long, cold winter . . . and so far a tough spring."

"Perhaps we could make a deal," Carlson offered.

Slade turned. Carlson smiled. "Come see me before you leave, after you've had your leisure time. I might have a proposition for you."

Chapter Eight

Slade's clothes arrived late in the afternoon. He tried them on and liked the fit. He dressed and considered his next move, tried to plot out a future course. One thing was sure. Until he had accumulated enough money to secure his freedom, he had to move on the run. He couldn't stay long in one place.

He looked smart in his tight black pants, his new white shirt with ruffles. He pulled on his socks and boots, hooked his gun belt on, adjusted it on his hip, and slipped into the black coat that hemmed out on his thighs. He tossed the water from his basin out the window. It splashed to the alley below. Then he filled the tin basin with cold water from a pitcher, dipped his hands in, and drew his fingers through his hair until it lay slick against his head.

The sun scattered a pink glow in the west as Slade walked out of the Carlson House. He thought he'd check things out, see if there was any way to make money. A lamplighter was firing up the naphtha lamps at the corners of Main Street.

Clusters of hide-hunters, trappers, and enlisted men from Fort Keogh gathered in front of the saloons. Two river men were discussing fishing as Slade passed them.

Miles City was like most of the small Western towns that had sprung up on the prairie around the Black Hills. It lived off the people who traded at the stores and patronized the saloons, dance halls, and parlor houses. Bull-whackers, mule skinners, buffalo hunters, prospectors on the move, men on the run from the law, loose women, hunters, and cattlemen—all were in evidence as Slade walked slowly down the board sidewalk. He passed the Merchants' and Drovers' Bank, which sat adjacent to the Cottage Saloon.

Slade had read in *Harper's Weekly* about the connecting door from the bank to the saloon and how the teller had a footplate on the floor attached to a pull wire that signaled the saloon in case of robbery. Last fall two men tried to rob the Merchants' and Drovers' and were overpowered by twenty to thirty men who poured into the bank from the saloon.

He smiled and walked on, past a parlor house, Ringer and Johnson's Livery Stable, "Red" Ward's Vaudeville House, Kitty Hardiman's Dance Hall.

Slade stopped at the Cosmopolitan Theatre and William Brown's Saloon, connecting establishments on the corner of Main Street just down from the Cottage Saloon. He hadn't seen a play or had any culture since he had left Deadwood. He remembered that it was at a play in Deadwood where he'd met Charlotte Adams, a young woman who had added a quality to his life he'd never known before.

Slade walked into the bar, had a drink, and bought a box ticket for the next performance at the Cosmopolitan. He went in and took his seat in a row of curtained boxes elevated around the main floor. A man in a vaudeville costume was onstage doing magic tricks.

"Like a drink, cowboy?" came a soft, suggestive voice.

Slade looked to his right, at the opening of the box, and saw a woman dressed in a bright red corset, tightly boned, with dark stockings held up by red garters. She wore red high-heels, and her lips were glossy red, her cheeks blushed, and her thick blond hair piled on top of her head in rolling curls.

She held a bottle of whiskey in one hand and her fingers dangled two glasses in the other.

"Sure," Slade said

"It's fifty cents a drink, a buck if I join you." The girl smiled, leaning forward, showing Slade her cleavage.

"Join me?" Slade said, a bit amazed.

"Sure. I can come in and spend some time, have a few drinks, watch the show with you . . . get acquainted, you know?"

"I think I do," Slade said. He fished out the money and paid.

"I'm JoAnne," the girl said. She drew the curtains so they pulled around the box and left only a small slit in front through which to see the show.

She sat down in the cushioned seat with Slade, poured drinks, and put the bottle on the floor. She sipped her drink and said, "Don't think I've seen you around here before."

Slade nodded.

Her hand slid over onto his thigh. She tapped her fingers slowly. "What's your name, honey?"

"Frank Slade."

"I could draw the curtains all the way closed, Frank, and you could have a good long kiss."

Slade had been hustled by saloon girls, but this was a new twist. "And I suppose that costs too?" He smiled.

"Sure. A girl's gotta live, Frank."

"I've been around the West awhile, but this is a new one for me," Slade said.

"I'm known as a box rustler. I can give you anything you want right here. Should I draw the curtains?"

Her hand slid over into Slade's crotch. She rubbed lightly, looked up at him, and smiled, her tongue slicking out, wetting her red lips.

Slade's member responded.

"Another drink?" JoAnne whispered, her hand fluttering to the white lace at the top of her corset. She dipped in, cupped her breasts and lifted them over the top of the lace.

"Like this?" she said, her voice husky, smoky. Her hand went back to Slade's thigh.

"Nice," Slade said.

"What about it then? Should I draw the curtains?" She got up, pulled the curtains together, poured two more drinks, and sat down.

"It's fifteen dollars," she said, "since it's early in the evening."

Slade lifted her hand from his thigh. He leaned over

and kissed her breasts. "A little too early for me," he whispered.

He peeled off two more dollars and got up.

"I work the parlor house down at Sixth and Main after the theater closes. You could drop by. Got liquor, dancing, and a professor that plays the piano."

"Maybe later," Slade said. He tossed the drink down and left the theater.

Dark had descended on Miles City. Slade walked back out onto the street. He felt like a card game. Maybe he could win a stake before he left town. He stopped at Charlie Brown's Saloon, walked in, and leaned into the bar. Loud noise filled his ears. Pungent smoke burned his nostrils. The piano player banged out "Clementine." Up on the stage women dancers tossed their skirts and showed off petticoats and stockings.

"Hello, stranger."

Slade turned. "Jesus! It's you, Jane. Calamity Jane! What are you doin' here?"

"Workin' the town. The big rush is over down in Deadwood."

Jane wore a frilly hat. Her hair banged out below the brim on her forehead. Slade opened his arms and she gave him a quick hug.

"And you?" she asked, breaking away. "I never thought I'd see you again, Frank Slade, not after Deadwood."

Slade related the events of the winter—hiding out, and his encounter with Taylor.

Martha Jane Canary smiled sympathetically. "Taylor's one of the crookedest, most low-down skunks in this part of hell," Jane said.

"He's straight now."

"You killed him?"

Slade took a drink of the trade bourbon from his shot glass. "I had to."

"And his wife got all the money you made in Deadwood?"

"She left me five hundred."

"Well," Jane said, taking a sip of whiskey, "you live and learn, as the saying goes, Slade."

"Yeah, and it's a tough lesson. I should have known better."

Jane finished her drink and leaned in closer to Slade. "I got some more bad news for you," she whispered.

The howl of men, the pounding piano, laughter, whooping, and singing filled the barroom. Jane grabbed Slade's bottle and poured a generous drink into a large barrel glass.

"It's about Deadwood," she said.

"I'm wanted there?" Slade smiled.

"Oh, the Kansas warrant is still out for you, Slade. And they found the Pueblo Kid dead. They knew you killed him, but there was no uproar about it 'cause everyone remembers you fondly—what you did for the people, takin' care of that gang of claim-jumpers from Chicago."

"So?"

"There was a fire."

"And . . ."

"Charlotte died."

Slade stiffened. It was as if a hot bolt of lightning had hit him.

Martha Jane put her arm around him.

"Dead?" Slade asked.

"It was a bad fire. Took her house while she was asleep."

"Shit," Slade mumbled.

"I talked to her after you left. She said you'd signed over the mining claim to her, but no one found it."

Slade grabbed the bottle, tipped it, and gurgled down two long shots. "Uh huh," he muttered.

"And Charlotte told me you put some money in the bank there."

"Yeah, the seventeen thousand I stole in Kansas."

"Well, the bank went down in the fire—one whole side of town burned down."

Slade took a deep breath and lifted his face, his chiseled chin pointed upward. He sighed, then relaxed back into the bar.

"There's more," Jane said.

Slade took a drink. Martha waited. "Go ahead," he said.

"There's a man named Holiday. Jubal Holiday. He came lookin' for you in Deadwood. Langdon down in Kansas sent him. Guess Langdon's the mayor of Dodge now. Anyway, this Holiday was still in town askin' questions about you when I left. He bought your mine for Langdon when it came up for sale after the fire."

The irony of his mine going to Langdon made Slade tremble. "This Holiday. Is he out of Texas?"

Jane nodded.

Slade knew of Holiday. Fast. Mean. Ruthless.

"And I suppose he's wearin' a badge?"

"Yes. Said he'd been hired by the state of Kansas to bring you back for murder and bank robbin'."

"Did he find out anything?"

"Charlotte had already died in the fire, and I refused to talk to him, but he's puttin' together a story. Folks talk enough."

"No one knew I headed north when I left Deadwood."

"He seems like he knows his business, Slade. He'll come lookin' for you."

"They've sent others," Slade said.

Slade and Jane stood in silence as the noise from the saloon got louder, more boisterous. They sipped whiskey slowly.

"Slade," Jane said, "what you have to learn in this acre of hell we live in is that you don't trust nobody."

Slade felt a rush of strength seep from his body. He suddenly felt tired, weak, depleted.

"What about you, Jane? Where you headed?"

"I'm gonna work some of the saloons here, then go back to Deadwood. That's my town. I like it. That's where I'll live and die. And you? What's your plan?"

"After what you told me, I guess I'll think on it. Stay here for a while. No one knows me. I need some money, another stake, then I'll head out to Yankton, catch a riverboat."

Calamity Jane looked up at Slade. "You ain't ever gonna get away from your past, Slade. You better figure on that right now."

Slade thought about it for a moment. "You might be right, but I'm not givin' in. I won't make an easy target, and I'll take some back-shooters with me."

Jane smiled. "I was hopin' you'd say somethin' like that, Slade."

She held out her hand. Slade took it and pulled her to him. Jane lifted up on the toes of her boots and pecked a kiss on his cheek.

"I got work to do," she whispered.

Slade let her go. She turned and walked through the crowd to a group of men near a poker table.

Chapter Nine

Calamity's news about Charlotte, his money, and the mining claim sent Slade back to his room at the Carlson House filled with rage and depression.

And now there was another gunfighter on his trail. He wondered if he would ever outlast Langdon and the trouble back in Kansas.

He packed up. If he left now he could get a good start on Holiday, maybe stay ahead of him long enough to lose him.

A knock came at his door.

Slade drew his Colt and slammed his body up against the wall at the side of the room, coiled, alert, ready.

"Mr. Slade? It's Carlson."

"Yeah?"

"Could you come down to my office? I'd like to talk."

"I'm not in the mood for talkin'."

"Could mean several thousand dollars for you."

Slade relaxed against the wall. He needed money to finance his travels. He unlocked the door and followed Carlson down the steps and through the lobby to another door that led to the back. Carlson opened it and Slade walked in.

"Jesus!" he exclaimed.

Carlson's living quarters were expensively appointed. The old man took Slade through a beautiful parlor with a huge Dominion piano in the corner, a big Acme Carbon parlor stove in the other. Rocking chairs sat side by side. A shadow box with cotton art inside hung above the pure horsehair couch. A bell jar stuffed with birds sat on a calling card table next to the couch.

"Here's an interesting chair," Carlson said, then demonstrated a chair that turned into a desk with one swing of the hinges.

Slade trailed Carlson through the kitchen, which had an expensive Wonder 817G Cook Stove with oven doors on both sides. A big iron teapot on top featured a turtle sprout. The table was already set with ivory-handled knives and forks.

Very plush, thought Slade. Money, big money.

Carlson finally led Slade into his study and bid him sit across a big oak desk from him. Slade slumped into the cowhide chair and pulled it closer to the desk, his hand loose at his side by his Peacemaker.

"Yes, I'm rich, If that's what's on your mind," Carlson said.

"It's obvious."

"Made it in Deadwood."

"Deadwood?" Slade said, intrigued. "I was in Deadwood and—"

"I was there long before you, Slade. Briefly, I'm from Boston. I was modestly successful there in banking, mostly stock issues."

Slade stiffened.

"I know, you're not a great admirer of bankers, but let me finish."

"You don't mind if I put my gun up on the desk," Slade said. He lifted his Peacemaker from his holster, pointed the long barrel at Carlson, and laid the gun on the desk. He rested his fingers near the weapon.

"That's not necessary, Mr. Slade, but if you feel more comfortable I'm agreeable."

"Continue," Slade said.

"I financed an expedition out of Sioux City into the Black Hills. This was two years before there even was a Deadwood, back when the Sioux still controlled the Black Hills."

"When the Black Hills was a sacred Sioux shrine."

"Back when the army was protecting it, when it was off-limits to white men."

"You went in after gold?" Slade asked.

"I didn't personally, but as I say, I financed an expedition that did."

"Lots of men tried to get into the Black Hills," Slade said, pulling out a cheroot. He fired it up.

"But they weren't organized and financed like my group. We got through the ring of soldiers. You'd be amazed, Mr. Slade. Huge nuggets the Sioux wouldn't touch. Gold nuggets lying along the streams, big chunks, just for the picking."

"And the army?"

"Escorted my expedition out on three different occasions, but my men hid the gold they'd found, and we kept going back in. Sometimes they didn't get to the Cottonwood, but when they did, we scored big.

"I moved to Sioux City to oversee the project. I guess by normal standards I was already an old man, in my fifties. Once the white man invaded the Black Hills, when the army couldn't stop them, we went back in and took out the gold we'd hidden.

"So, you stole the Sioux's gold," Slade drawled.

"Please, Mr. Slade. The Sioux didn't want it. They refused to touch that gold."

"So, you stole their gold," Slade repeated.

"Slade, if it hadn't been me, it would have been someone else. It was an investment project, and I did make millions, but I would assure you that other men have pilfered much more."

Slade puffed his cheroot and nodded. "I reckon you're right about that."

"You went there, I understand, when it was still illegal. You made money mining that gold."

"And I reckon you're right about that, too," Slade agreed.

"I took the gold, came here last year to Miles City, and built this hotel, decided to settle down and enjoy wealth, enjoy life, get away from the city."

"It's a nice story, Carlson, real interesting, but what does this have to do with me?"

"Concerns my daughter."

"How's that?"

"My wife died. My daughter, Calla, went to college. I wanted her to travel when she finished, go to Europe, find a baron, a prince, but she insisted on joining me here in the Montana Territory. What could I do? I let her come out. She was going to run the hotel for me.

She was a smart, beautiful young woman. Went to William and Mary College.''

''Was?''

''That's what I wanted to discuss with you, Slade. You see, she disappeared a few months ago. Simply disappeared. I have no reason to think she'd run away since she wanted to come out here so badly. So, I believe she was taken.''

''Kidnapped?'' Slade asked.

''If you like.''

''Someone who wants ransom?''

''That's what I thought at first, but there's been no demand, no word, so I've decided against that.''

''What then?''

''First, I don't think she ran away.''

''Not from this setup,'' Slade said. ''So, what do you think?''

''You've heard about the big copper strikes over near Butte, the silver and gold strikes around Virginia City?''

''Sure.''

''There was a big silver strike a few months back southwest of Bozeman, down in the Tobacco Root Mountains near Virginia City. It's called Silver Creek. I wager it'll be one of those towns that's here today and gone tomorrow—won't even be recorded on the history maps—but they've hit it big.''

''I've heard of it,'' Slade said.

''There's a man down there named Brady. He owns mines, saloons, gambling halls, and he owns women.''

''Women?''

''This is what I hear. I hear he has several beautiful women who work his saloons.''

"Women working saloons in a mining town is nothing new, Mr. Carlson."

"But these are very young, very beautiful women, not the usual type for a saloon hustler."

"And you think maybe your daughter is there in Silver Creek?"

"Precisely. She's young and beautiful. I think my Calla's in Silver Creek." Carlson handed Slade a picture of Calla. Slade was impressed. The girl in the photo had regal beauty, she was young, and she radiated class.

"And you think she's being held against her will?" Slade asked.

"Yes, by this man named Brady. I want you to go find out if she's there. If she is, I want you to bring her back safely."

"Why don't you contact the law?"

"I understand Brady controls the law there, the sheriff and the courts."

"Not unusual," Slade said.

"Look, Slade. I'm gettin' on in years. I had Calla late in life. I probably haven't been the father I should have been. I can't travel. My body won't take it. Every man I've sent there has disappeared, just like Calla."

"I hear Daly and Clark have interests in that area," Slade said.

"They have interests wherever there's money, Slade, but they seem like semi-honest men. They're more interested in politics and which one will be governor."

"So, you want me to check things out in Silver Creek?"

"Right."

"And the deal?"

"Five hundred now, five thousand if you bring Calla back."

Slade butted his cigar in the ashtray, then relit it. He took a deep pull and blew a cloud of smoke.

"Not enough. I have other plans," Slade said.

"Six hundred and six thousand."

"Seven-fifty now and seventy-five hundred if I bring your daughter back."

"Fine, fine." Carlson smiled happily. He rose from his plush chair and went to the black safe in the corner behind his desk. He spun the dial and took out a bag of gold coins.

Slade stood up and holstered his gun. "You'll have to buy me a horse and some gear, that'll be a hundred extra."

"Fine," Carlson said, counting the gold coins into stacks on his desk.

"Why me?" Slade asked. "Is it because of the gunfight with Taylor and his men?"

"No, not at all. It's because of what Calamity Jane told me about you."

Slade smiled and whispered, "Ah, that Jane, there's a real woman, a real woman."

Carlson chuckled and extended his hand. "A deal then?"

"Deal," Slade said.

Chapter Ten

"You'd like this 'puddin' foots,'" the livery
owner said.

"Percheron's a good horse for the
plains, but I'm headed into the mountains along the
way," Slade answered. "I need an Appaloosa."

"Got only one."

"The blue roan with the dark spots on his rump?"

"Yup, he's seventy bucks."

"I'll try him," Slade said.

"Goin' down to the Big Horns, the Absarokas? Maybe
the Tobacco Roots?"

"Could be one of those ranges," Slade said.

"Sure. Then this is the mount you want."

Slade paid, threw an Ellenberg saddle on the horse,
and cinched up. He stopped at Hubbell's and bought a
new Levi's outfit—black pants, blue chambray shirt, and
black jacket. He rode his new horse to the Carlson House

and picked up his gear. Carlson had sent out to the store for some jerky, bacon, corn, and coffee. He had it wrapped neatly in buffalo skin for Slade.

"You'll need some nourishment," the old man said.

Slade put the grub in his roll and left as the sun set over Miles City. He rode down the Bozeman Trail, along the Yellowstone River, past Honsinger Hill, and made the small settlement of Forsyth by nightfall the next day. He avoided the town and camped on the west edge of the river.

Slade stayed alert for possible Indian attacks. The Nez Percé were retreating into Idaho, but many of them had decided to make a stand in Montana. One last battle. The Nez Percé had a reputation for fighting and bravery, so Slade was careful.

The next morning, refreshed from a stick of jerky and some parched corn, Slade rode past Fort Pease, Junction City, and Custer, all situated at the confluence of the Yellowstone and Big Horn Rivers.

Slade camped down at dusk on the Yellowstone near Pompy's Tower, an amazing piece of rock that jutted up off the prairie like a ship stuck in time.

He walked across the rugged sand to the butte, circled the bald hunk of rock, and was surprised to find an inscription carved by Captain William Clark back in July of 1806 when the Lewis and Clark Expedition had pushed through looking for an opening to the sea.

Slade rolled a cigarette, lit it, and stood in awe of the huge rock. He was impressed that Lewis and Clark had been through this same part of the West seventy-one years before him, searching for a river route to the Pacific Ocean.

Slade walked back to his horse, watered him, combed

him, massaged his neck, and tethered him to a tree. The big Appaloosa snorted appreciation.

He brushed the horse and thought about the Indians retreating ahead of him. He had read in the Yellowstone *Journal* how troops from Fort Ellis, near Bozeman, had been driving the Nez Percé across the border into Idaho and north into Canada.

Slade carried his saddle to a group of boulders along the river and settled in for the night. He dug a pit with his hand spade, clustered some rocks around it, then gathered driftwood for a small fire.

He constructed a wigwam of twigs, laid on some driftwood, struck a lucifer, and watched the orange flame dance into a hot fire.

Slade filled his coffeepot from the river, boiled the water over the fire, and made some coffee. He sat back against a boulder, rustled some jerky from his pack, and munched while he sipped the steaming java.

The night was warm. A soft breeze rolled off the rush of the river. The cottonwood branches swished above him. The sky was a blanket of blue lights.

Slade finished eating and lay back on his saddle, his Winchester propped against a rock next to him. He lit a quirly cigarette and inhaled the sweet smoke. Lady Fortuna had smiled on him again in the face of the old man Carlson. If he could find Carlson's daughter and bring her back, he'd have another stake. He decided not to think further than that. If he was successful, if he got the money, then he'd plan his next move . . . maybe back to the Black Hills, south to Cheyenne, west to California, down to Nevada.

Slade slept lightly, alert in a half doze, waking often

to the sounds of birds, animals, and an occasional crack of thunder. He was up and ready to ride before dawn.

He followed the Bozeman Trail along the Yellowstone. Flat country. Lonely. Desolate. Empty. He rode hard all the way to Coulson, a small trading post that would soon change its name to Billings. He made camp and spent another uneventful night.

The next morning he ran into a scouting party of Nez Percé. He was riding a curve in the Yellowstone where the Stillwater River flowed south into the Absaroka Mountains.

They were waiting for him on the bend near the confluence. Slade leapt from his horse and ran to the edge of the river. He found a log and jumped behind it, lying flat on his belly, his Winchester ready, the barrel leveled over the log.

He counted seven braves. Slade had never encountered the Nez Percé before, but he knew they had gained a reputation for marksmanship in fights with General Miles.

They rode hard right at Slade.

He cocked the Winchester, levered a shell into the chamber, and fired a warning shot over the Indians' heads. They kept coming. Slade aimed at the lead brave and squeezed off another shot. The Indian flew off the horse backward, legs stretched out in a wide V.

The other braves fired at full gallop, something Slade had never seen before. They shot at him over the back and under the neck of their horses. He ducked, his face slamming down into the sandy dirt along the river. A hail of bullets shaved chips of wood from the log. Slade bobbed back up and aimed.

The Indians were reloading, still at full gallop. He

saw one brave slosh a charge of powder from his powder-horn, then spit a ball from his mouth into the gun's muzzle loader. The brave swung under the neck of his horse and fired. The others also reloaded as they charged.

This was new to Slade, and frightening—Indians shooting and reloading at full gallop. He fired ten quick shots, the lever of his rifle in a hot blur. Two Indians dropped from their horses. Another tumbled from his pony wounded. Slade shot him again, then took a slug in his shoulder. Quick pain, hot numbness. He pumped off three more shots and two braves went down.

The last brave, blood squishing from holes in his buckskin jacket, his gun loose on his fingers, leapt from his horse. He ran at Slade, yelling insanely.

"Jesus!" Slade shouted. He'd counted off fifteen shots in his Winchester. He knew it was empty. He stood up and drew the .45. The Indian dropped his gun, charged to within ten feet of Slade, and tossed a tomahawk, then pulled a knife and leapt. Frank shot him, dropped the bleeding brave at his feet. The Indian made a valiant attempt to rise. He clutched at Slade's legs, pulled himself to his knees, grunted loudly, and slumped to the ground. Slade kicked him away and took a deep breath. He stumbled backward to the log and sat down. His wound hurt. A slug had grazed the top of his left shoulder.

Slade ripped his shirt open and walked to the river. He dipped the shirt in the water and washed the wound, then opened his canteen of whiskey and poured a generous slosh onto the cut.

"Oooo, jeeezzzuz!" he yelped as a bone-shaking pain thundered through him.

The sun was hot now. Slade sat on the log and let the

rays warm and clot the wound, then he made a bandage of his shirt and applied it to his shoulder. He pulled a new shirt from his travel bag and put it on.

One thing for sure, Slade didn't want to meet anymore Nez Percé. He'd never seen Indians shoot and reload at full speed, and he didn't want to see it again.

Ever.

Chapter Eleven

Slade decided to travel by moonlight. He reloaded his rifle, mounted, and galloped down the river-bank at full speed looking for a thick grove of cottonwoods where he could hide until dark.

He rode until he came to a horseshoe in the Yellow-stone with a thick cluster of trees. Slade yanked on the reins and turned the Appaloosa into the trees. He nosed the big horse around the trunks to a clearing.

His shoulder had stiffened. A stinging pain screamed up his neck and down his arm. He dismounted, pulled the saddle from the horse, and tethered the animal to a tree. He dragged his saddle to some bushes and made a place for himself.

Slade cocked the Winchester and laid it over his knee, then took his Colt Peacemaker out of the holster and put it beside him. He pulled an old *Harper's* magazine from his travel bag and lay back to read while the sun splashed healing rays on his shoulder.

He'd purchased the *Harper's* months before in Medora, up in northern Dakota. He was interested in the feature on Montana and the copper industry.

Slade turned the page and found a story about copper being used to transmit spoken words. It had been tried successfully the year before, in 1876. The writer, Dick Goodbody, raved about how Butte, Montana, was emerging as a big copper producer. The story told about the varied used of copper, and ventured that soon copper would be used to generate electric light.

He read on about William J. Parks, who was mining silver near Butte. Parks, with meager equipment and mining by himself, had struck copper ore at a depth of 150 feet. *Harper's* said the ore was so pure it could be shipped to "hell and back for smelting" and make a profit.

The story profiled William A. Clark, who had formed the Colorado and Montana Smelting Company at Butte to provide a local market for copper.

The Anaconda, originally claimed in the fall of 1875 by Michael Hickey, was already producing copper. Marcus Daly had examined the property and taken an option on it for its silver content.

Hickey had needed financing, so the story went, and had turned to George Hearst, J.B. Haggin, and Lloyd Tevis.

"Shit," Slade mumbled. "Those were the same bastards who claimed the Homestake Gold Mine in Deadwood and nudged everyone else out of the picture."

Slade continued reading, turning the pages, wondering about this new rush to copper in Montana. Maybe

Butte would be his next stop. "They probably don't even now how to refine it," he said to himself.

Slade laid the magazine down and lit a cheroot. *Copper!* More precious than gold or silver? Did it hold potential for a man like Slade? But then he remembered Carlson. He had a job to do in Silver Creek, a verbal contract with Carlson, and he meant to keep his word. Slade figured he could check out Butte and the copper discovery later.

He lay back on his saddle and dozed off. The sun was dipping deep into the prairie when Slade decided to move on. He pushed the Appaloosa through the night, and arrived near Bozeman before sunup.

The small settlement was set against the Bridger Mountains. He rode through the Valley of Flowers and down into Bozeman, a town named for John Bozeman, a man who'd made his name leading wagon trains of immigrants from the East to the silver and gold strikes in Montana.

Slade rode the Bozeman Trail right into town, found a livery stable and quartered his horse, then walked to the Bozeman Hotel. He rang the bell and waited.

A woman in a white cloth calico dress with bright designs on the front swept into the lobby. Slade turned and watched her walk to the counter. She had plush, ample hips and a round face with thick lips. She was older, maybe forty, but she had a young demeanor and was fine-looking.

"Would you like to engage a room, sir?"

Slade nodded. "And a doctor to look at my shoulder."

"Have a skirmish with the Nez Percé?"

"You could say that."

"They're defeated, but they won't give up. Got no sense, those Indians."

The woman walked behind the counter and gazed Slade up and down as if he were a fat cow at market.

"I can have Doc Thomas come over and look at that shoulder," she said.

"I'd be obliged, ma'am."

"Where you headed?" the woman asked.

"The Tobacco Root Mountains, a place called Silver Creek. I need directions."

"Down to the silver strike, huh?"

Again Slade nodded.

"Sure. You ride southwest down near Virginia City, along the Gallatin River. Just take the Bridger Pass out of town."

"Bridger Pass?"

"Named for Jim Bridger. He was first out here with the immigrant miners, but Bozeman got all the publicity."

"A room?" Slade persisted.

"Sure, two-fifty gold. Don't take paper money."

Slade gave her a gold coin.

"Up the stairs, second floor, it's on the corner. No one will bother you there."

Slade dragged his gear up the stairs to the room. The walls were paper thin, the bed had a soiled coverlet on it, and the room smelled like dust.

Slade locked the door, dumped his gear on the floor by the bed, and opened the window. He unhooked his gun belt, pulled the Colt from the holster, and lay back on the old brass bed. The thin mattress felt good after several days on the Appaloosa. Slade took a deep breath, clutched the .45, and relaxed.

A knock at the door sent him jumping form the bed. He knelt down, both hands cradling the Colt.

"It's me, Donna," came the woman's voice.

Slade got up and unlocked the door, then stood back, gun ready.

"Jesus, you're nervous," Donna said, entering the room carrying a tray. "I couldn't get the doc. He had to go to the Crazy Mountains north of here. There's a pox goin' 'round up there. But I got some pure alcohol and some cotton dobs. I can fix that wound for you."

She fanned out a hand and pushed Slade onto the bed. He slid back to the edge, back straight, gun ready.

"Relax. I ain't gonna hurt you," Donna said. "Lemme see that wound."

She ripped Slade's shirt off and pinched open the deep cut on his shoulder.

"Shit!" Slade yelped.

"I know, I know, hurts like hell, but hold on," Donna whispered.

She sat down beside Slade, placed the tray on the bed, and sloshed alcohol into the wound. Slade gritted his teeth and huffed a low moan.

"That's the worst. Now I'll clean it real good and dress it with a clean wrap."

Donna worked quickly and professionally, tying a white bandage across Slade's shoulder and hooking it under his armpit. "Let that settle in. Tomorrow take the wrapping off and it'll heal nice."

Slade drew a long breath and lay back on the bed, his boots flat on the floor, his knees cocked apart. His chest heaved.

"I never did make you sign in," Donna said. "What's your name?"

"Slade, Frank Slade."

He lifted off the mattress, tried to get up. Donna pushed him back. "Just lay there."

She took the tray to the chiffonier and turned to Slade. "You don't look like the usual kind of man that comes through here, Slade. What's your deal?"

"What's that mean?" Slade questioned.

"Most of the men come through are grizzly, dirty, uncouth, most heading for the silver strikes south of here."

She sat down again by Slade. Her hand slid into Slade's hair. "Tobacco Mountains, huh? Silver Creek?"

"Yes," said Slade.

"Got business there?"

"I might."

Donna's hand slipped in a curve over Slade's thigh. "Brady owns that town," she whispered, pressing down closer to Slade.

"That's what I hear."

"You can let go of that six-shooter. I ain't gonna hurt you," Donna whispered huskily.

Her hand fluttered to Slade's crotch. She rubbed and teased until his cock responded.

"Mmmm, that feels good, real good," Donna said.

"I don't think I'm up to this," Slade mumbled.

Donna rose up, looked down into Slade's handsome face, his brown eyes, and smiled. "Oh yeah? I'd say you are."

She unbuttoned his jeans and yanked around inside his fly, finally tugging out his fleshy erection. She gasped. "I knew you was different," she said, her hand clutching his cock.

She lifted Slade's Colt from his hand, held the barrel

on her lips. Her tongue licked over the top as she looked down at him, still gripping his hardness.

"Jesus," Slade mumbled.

Donna dropped his Peacemaker on the bed, stood up, lifted her skirt, and straddled Slade, taking him in. She rotated, undulated on top of him.

"You owe me for takin' care of that wound," she whispered.

Slade lay back and relaxed. "I reckon you're right about that," he said.

The moon hung like a jagged hunk of silver as Jubal Holiday rode into Miles City. It was late. He stopped at the Carlson House and checked in.

He followed Jedediah to a room. When Jed turned, Holiday held out a ten-dollar gold coin. "I'm lookin' for a man named Slade. He pass this way?"

Jedediah's eyes studied the muscular gunfighter, his dusty jeans, his lawman jacket. He saw the badge.

"Slade?"

"Yeah, Frank Slade," Holiday said, dropping the coin into Jedediah's outstretched hand. "Know anything about him?"

"Maybe."

Holiday waited. "Well?"

Jed knew he'd lose his job if Carlson ever found out he'd spilled his guts. He kept his hand out. Holiday deposited another coin.

"Slade, you say?"

"Get on with it," Jubal snapped.

"Frank Slade left here several days ago, headed west."

"Where's he going?"

"Can't say. Just know he rode west along the Yellowstone."

Jubal Holiday gave the old man a tired smile.

"You'll keep it to yourself I said anything," Jedediah whispered.

"And you won't mention I asked after him, right?"

Jed nodded.

Jubal went to his room and locked the door. He lay back on the bed. His body ached. "I'm gettin' old," he mumbled. "Never hurt like this before, just from riding."

He dozed off. In the morning Jubal would get up and do fifty fast draws in the mirror.

A manhunter had to stay in shape.

Chapter Twelve

The next morning Slade got up, washed, and walked down to the lobby. Donna sat in a wicker chair near the door.

"Just stay on the Bozeman Trail, go up over Bridger Pass. The land flattens out down near the Gallatin River. Go southwest into the Tobacco Roots, ride along the river . . . you'll find Silver Creek."

Slade dipped into his saddlebags and handed a gold coin to Donna.

She stood up and watched Slade walk down the sidewalk. The morning was fresh, clean. Slade turned. Donna waved. He nodded and walked to the livery stable.

It was a tough pull over the Bridger Pass, but as Donna had said, once he was over the mountain, the long slope melted into flat prairie.

Slade followed the trail a short distance out of Boze-man until he came to the Gallatin River. He turned the Appaloosa south, started down into the Tobacco Root Mountains, and followed the flat land on the west side of the river across from the jutting peaks of the rising stone mountains on the other side.

He made camp for the night along the Gallatin, then rode to Silver Creek the next morning. The creek shot out of the Gallatin to the southwest, heading in the direction of Yellowstone Park.

.The new mining town was strung out for two miles along the creek in a deep gulch. It reminded Slade of Deadwood. Men were living in dugouts, wagons, tents, caves, and wickiups of alder and pine boughs. Some miners simply camped out on their blankets. But as Slade continued along the creek he saw the new construction. Lumber from the sawmill in Bannack had been brought in and buildings were going up.

Slade trotted his Appaloosa and watched men work the creek sidebars. The tributary gulches had been pros-pected extensively and claims staked. A stream mill cranked in the distance. Circles of men knelt in the stream sloshing pans in arcs, hurling out the dirt and silica quartz; they held magnets over the layers left in the pan and pulled out the fine specks of gold.

Slade lifted a vial of mink oil from his pack, pulled his .45, and applied the thick gel to his holster. He wanted to be ready.

He passed through a shanty town, then into the main section of Silver Creek. He rode slowly past a big, new saloon called the Golden Nugget, past the Witherspoon Hotel, the Silver Bar Café, and another new saloon, gambling hall, and hotel named the Regal. The new, expensive places probably belonged to Brady, Slade conjectured.

He reined in at a rail in front of the Durango Saloon, a cheap wooden structure, and pushed through the batwing doors. He walked to a makeshift bar of oak planks laid over barrels.

Slade leaned in. "Got any Sweet Home whiskey?"

The bartender gave him a good laugh. "Shit, mister, you must think you're in Denver or Cheyenne. I got tangleroot and straight trade whiskey here. Not the best, but I'm the cheapest in town. You go down to Brady's joints and they'll take your leg for Sweet Home."

Slade ordered a bottle of trade whiskey, pulled the cork, and poured a shot. The warm, amber liquid slid down his throat and splashed into his belly. It felt good. He poured another, gulped it, then checked out the room.

A group of miners were gathered around a poker table in the back. Three women stood behind the men.

Slade rolled a cigarette and sipped whiskey. The group at the table argued about a man named Harper. Slade looked them over and listened.

A young girl drew his attention. She was thin, but sexy, and her white silk blouse and black calico skirt hugged her body in a way that told a man she knew what she was about.

"This Harper they're discussing," Slade said to the bartender, "what's his connection to these people?"

"He works for Brady, helps Brady take over these folk's mines."

"Claim-jumping?"

"No, Brady uses the apex law."

Slade had never heard of a law that allowed a man to take another man's claim. "Apex law?"

"It's on the books, mister, but don't ask me about it. I ain't no barrister. I'm tryin' to hang on runnin' this saloon. All I know is that when folks find a vein, Brady ends up with it. That's what they're talkin' about. They've formed an association."

It had been a long ride. Slade's butt was sore. He sipped slowly at the whiskey, and even though it was trade booze, he liked the lift it gave him. He thought about Carlson back in Miles City, about his daughter Calla, and Carlson's suspicion that she was in Silver Creek working for Brady.

The bat-wing door slammed open. A short man dressed in a gray three-piece suit walked in. He wore a new black Stetson. He had a double gun rig strapped low on his hips, and was followed by two other men.

The bartender retreated to the end of the bar. The miners stopped talking.

The short man walked to the middle of the saloon. "Time you folks break up this meetin'. Ain't no way you're gonna do business with this cooperative of yours."

A tall miner stood up. "We've had enough of you, Harper. Enough of you and Brady stealin' our mines."

Harper smiled. "Now ain't that too bad. We never stole a claim yet. Everything we done has been legal."

"Sit down, Caleb," a woman said. "Let him be."

"No, I ain't sittin' down. It's time we let Brady and his men know we're gonna fight back."

The miner was no match for Harper. His gun was old, his rig worn. Frank set his shot glass on the bar and leaned back against the planks.

The pretty young girl who had caught Slade's attention rushed to the tall miner. "No, Daddy, don't!"

"Get back, Denise," her father growled.

Harper's lips curled into a sinister smile. He wore a black vest with his gray suit. His eyes were set back deep under a jutting forehead.

"Nice-lookin' daughter you got there, Rafferty. She's ripe for sure. Me and the boys here, we've been talkin' about her a lot lately. We think she'd be good in the sack."

The miner trembled with anger. His hand shook as it wavered over his holster. Slade moved away from the bar. He smelled big trouble. Harper's smile faded. His arm curled and his hand looked eager to draw.

Slade walked out from the bar. "That's no way to talk to a young lady," he said calmly.

Harper ignored him. "Yeah, she looks real good. Me and the boys been admirin' her for a long time."

Slade took a step toward Harper. Harper finally looked at him. "Out of the way, cowboy. This ain't got nothin' to do with you."

Slade held his position.

The girl stood beside her father, frightened, pulling on his arm. "Daddy, come sit down."

"Yeah, sit down, and you folks go back out to your camp. Forget about this cooperative you dreamed up," Harper said.

The miner refused to budge.

"Please, Daddy," the young girl pleaded.

"You should take her advice," Harper said, "and you should keep her out of town. Young girl like her, with a great butt like that, gets my men all hopped up."

Slade stood off to the side between the two men,

watching both of them. "Leave the girl out if it, just back up and leave!" he shouted.

"And who would you be, cowboy? This new miners' association bring you in to fight their battles?"

"You owe the young lady an apology," Slade said.

Harper laughed, then drew. His gun blurred, but Slade had already greased up with mink oil. He fired and hit Harper in the chest. The two men with Harper went for their guns. Slade nicked one on the wrist. The other dropped his gun back into his holster.

Harper fell to his knees. He raised his gun at Slade. Frank squeezed off another shot that cut through Harper's neck. Blood spurted. He looked up at Slade, his mouth unhinged, his eyes glazed.

"Damn," he burbled, then he slumped over and curled slowly to the floor.

Slade leveled his Peacemaker at Harper's men. They backed off.

"Get this scum out of here," Slade hissed.

Harper's men pulled their dead leader across the saloon to the bat-wing doors.

Silence.

Slade walked back to the bar, holstered his gun. and finished his drink. The man named Caleb and the girl named Denise looked at him with puzzled gazes.

Caleb walked up. "Look, mister, that was some fine shootin', but it was my fight."

"And you'd be dead right now," Slade said.

"He's right, Daddy," the young girl said, as she rushed toward Caleb and Slade.

Caleb relaxed, stuck out his hand. "Caleb Rafferty. I'm head of the miners' association."

Frank gave him his name and shook his hand.

"Come join us for a drink," Caleb said.

Slade looked at the miner, then his daughter. She had sparkling green eyes, full cheeks. Her tight blouse revealed small but firm breasts.

He followed them to their table. Caleb introduced Slade to the miners. "We're part of the miners' association, Mr. Slade. We formed up to fight men like Harper."

"And the man called Brady?" Slade asked.

"Yes. He's been stealin' our mines. Every time we hit a new vein, make a new strike, he takes over. He uses the apex law."

"The bartender mentioned it."

"Look, mister," one of the miners said, "Billy Harper was Brady's fastest gun. You took him. We could use a man like you on our side."

"That's for true," Caleb said.

"You have business here in Silver Creek, Mr. Slade?" the young girl asked.

"Just passing through," Slade lied.

"We could be in a position to make you an offer to stay around," Caleb said.

"Help you against Brady?"

"We could use someone with a fast gun like yours. Throw a scare into Brady and his bunch. Scare 'em like they been doin' us."

Slade sat down. He already had one job, but the prospect of another intrigued him. "You folks know more about this man Brady than I do. I'm interested, if you think I can help, but I understand he does things legally with the apex law."

"That's just it," another miner said. "He does it legally, but it ain't legal, that's the way we see it."

"No one's gone up against Harper before," said another miner. "You done him in. Brady will be gunnin' for you anyway. You might just as well join us."

Slade hedged. "Let me think about it."

Caleb leaned his elbows on the table, pushed forward. "We could offer you a good salary for a gun like that."

Slade glanced at the young girl. She stared at him with the sparkling green eyes and nodded as if to say, "Take the deal."

"I just got into town, let me think about it," Slade said.

"We're out in Crooked Gulch," Caleb said. "When you decide, come out, talk to us."

A miner pushed a shot glass full of whiskey over to Slade. He curled his fingers around it, lifted the shooter, then gulped it down.

"I'll get back to you," Slade said, getting up. He excused himself properly to the women and walked to the bar.

The miners buzzed for a few minutes at the table, then they filed out of the saloon.

Slade watched the pretty young girl. Harper had been right about one thing—she had a great butt and it waved deliciously under the thin calico. She disappeared through the door and Slade turned back to the bar. He had some thinking to do.

He was in Silver Creek to see if Carlson's daughter was being held by Brady, but maybe he could combine the job with the miner's offer.

Things were looking up.

Chapter Thirteen

S lade unhitched his horse and walked him down the dusty main street. He moved around the buckboards and buggies, reading the signs on the new wooden buildings as he looked for the livery stable.

Farmer & Wells
Attorneys At Law
Practice in all courts of the territory
Special Attention Given To
Contests and Appeals

F.W. COOPER
Restaurant and Lunch Room
Dealer in Choice Confectionary, Foreign and Domestic
Fruits, Nuts, Cigars, Tobaccos, Etc.
Meals and Lunch served at all hours. **Try Us**

J. W. THAYER
Dealer in Pure
Drugs & Medicines
Chemicals, Paints, Oils, Pencils, Wall Paper, Toilet and
Fancy Goods and all other goods found in a first class
DRUGSTORE

Hank Black
LIVERY STABLE
We have robes and brushes
WE CARE ABOUT YOUR HORSE

Slade pulled his Appaloosa into Hank Black's Livery
and asked about a hotel.

"Mr. Brady has the best," Black said.

"Anything else?" Slade asked.

"The Wheeler House, right up the street at the end."

Slade took his possibles and walked to the Wheeler
House. It was new, but cheaply built. He paid for five
nights with a half-eagle gold piece, hauled his belong-
ings to the end of the second floor, and turned to the
hotel clerk. "This will do," he said.

The old man stood in the doorway. "You'll want a
bath, I reckon."

Slade nodded.

"I'll have the maid boil up some water and fill the
tub. It's halfway down the hall on the right."

Slade tipped the clerk and closed the door. He checked
the bed. It was soft, and he felt as though he could sleep
for a week. He pulled off his boots, and stripped down
to his balbriggans. He lighted a cheroot and took his
valuables to the bath with him.

An old oak tub awaited him, the hot water steaming.

Slade sliped out of his shorts and slid into the tub. the warm water felt good. He relaxed, his Colt on an ax barrel next to the tub.

Slade chomped on the cigar and let the hot water caress his aching body. He scrubbed down, soaked, and smoked, then finally emerged from the tub, dripping in suds. He toweled and slipped into a clean pair of Levi's, threw the towel around his neck, and walked back to his room. He unlocked the door and lay back on the clean bed for a light snooze.

A knock interrupted his nap. Slade rolled off the bed with his Peacemaker and grumbled, "Yeah?"

"It's Denise, Mr. Slade."

"Who?"

"Caleb's daughter."

Slade opened the door and the girl walked in. She stood in the middle of the room, pretty, young, and radiant. Slade closed the door.

"Sorry to invade on you like this," she said.

Slade motioned to a wooden chair near the chiffonier. She walked over and sat down. Slade sat on the edge of the bed, still holding his .45.

"I stayed behind," she said. "I wanted to thank you for standing up for me, for saving my pa's life like you did."

Slade gazed at her fine shape, her shiny black boots, black skirt, and tight silk blouse. Her brown hair fell in soft curls on her shoulders. Her square-cut face glowed with a farm-fresh innocence.

Denise returned his admiring gaze, her green eyes full of emotion as they gazed over his lean six-three frame, his naked shoulders, muscular stomach, and dark tanned face.

"How old are you?" Slade asked.

"Old enough."

"Young," Slade murmured.

"Not young like you think," Denise said. She stood up, walked to the bed, and stood before Slade, her hands on her hips in a challenge, her chin jutting. "Besides, you're not that old yourself, I can tell."

"Twenty-eight," Slade confessed.

"See? That's not so old."

Denise sat down on the bed beside Slade. She smelled good. Her shoulder, the thin silk of her blouse, brushed against his arm.

"We need help, Mr. Slade," she whispered, turning on the bed, facing him. "The strikes the miners have been hitting out in Crooked Gulch could make everyone rich, but it's not workin' out that way."

Her hand reached out. She touched Slade's arm and drew a finger down his bicep, over his elbow.

"Are you flirting with me?"

She smiled and offered her lips for a kiss. Slade slid an arm around her, pulled her close, and kissed her full and hard on her ripe mouth.

Her hand dropped to his thigh.

She broke off the kiss and whispered. "I'd like to show you my appreciation." Her eyes glanced down at the curling bulge in Slade's Levi's. Her hand slid between his legs.

"God," she gasped.

Slade kissed her again, pushed her back on the bed, then stood up and took his Levi's off.

Denise lay with her brown hair splashed on the pillow. Slade stood naked over the bed, his cock rigid and long. Denise stared at the thick hardness. Her mouth formed a little red O. She reached up and fisted him. Her fingers curled around the stalk. She pulled him down on top of her. Slade lifted her black skirt and unbuttoned her blouse. His lips circled the tiny nipples on her little breasts, and his hand slid into her moist softness.

Her chemisette was damp between her legs. Slade rubbed tenderly.

"I shouldn't . . . I shouldn't be lettin' you do this, Slade," Denise whispered, "but I wanted to show . . ."

Slade took his hand away.

"No, don't!"

"But . . ."

"I shouldn't let you, but I want you to."

Slade angled his hand back into the oozing warmth and felt her unique offering. His mouth worked the erect nipples of her boobs, which had heaved forward like ripe fruit.

He lifted off. "I can stop," he said.

"No, I don't want you to stop."

Slade took a deep breath. "But you didn't come here just for this, did you?"

"No, but we can talk about the rest later," Denise said, opening her legs farther apart.

Slade pulled her chemisette down her thighs, over her knees, and took it off. Her hand continued to clutch him.

"It feels good," she whispered. "Feels good in my hand like that."

"What did you want to tell me?" Slade asked, his hand still busy between her legs.

"That can wait."

Slade rolled over and mounted the young girl. She

held him like a vise. He pushed and his hard shaft slid into her.

"Ohhh, gawwwd!" Denise whimpered.

He thumped up and down slowly. She huffed a long hot sigh. Her legs opened wider, and she circled them around Slade, hooked him in.

Slade began a hard pump as he slid deep into Denise's tight sheath. She wrapped her arms around his neck, pulled his head down, and kissed him wildly on the lips.

"We can stop now," Slade offered, breaking the kiss. "You're young, you can change your mind."

"Shut up and fuck me!" Denise hissed.

Slade didn't want to take advantage of such a young lady, but her lewd call for action spurred him to a faster stroke. He humped up and down and she took the full force of his hard hammering.

Slade slid his hand under Denise and felt her fabulous rump. She lifted off the bed to give him room for a good grip. Her legs tightened around him. Her arms locked his shoulders. She bounced up and down.

"God, this feels good," she said. "I've never felt this good."

Then it happened. Slade stroked faster, harder. Denise met his pumping with wild undulations. Her breath caught in her throat as though she were about to stifle a scream. Her body shook. Slade pounded. She shuddered.

"Oh, oh, jeeeez, Slade. Oh, God!"

Slade poured into her. Denise stiffened, then slumped back onto the bed huffing and puffing, catching her breath.

Slade fell on top of her. He licked her ear and her

neck, slid an arm under her neck, pulled her up and kissed her again, then released her and rolled off.

He lay beside her, waiting for her to speak first, to tell him what she was doing in his room, why she had opened her young charms to him.

Back in Miles City, in the glow of an oil lamp, Jubal Holiday stood in front of the chiffonier mirror, his gun strapped low on his hip.

He drew, set, fired.

When he'd done fifty draws he headed down the stairs for a meal.

Old man Carlson watched Jubal stroll through the lobby. It had to be the man Calamity Jane had told him about. What could he do? There was no way to warn Slade.

But something told Carlson Slade knew Holiday was on his trail, and if what he'd heard about Slade was true, the young fugitive would be ready for Holiday.

Jubal went to the Bannister Café, ordered a stack of pancakes, a slice of ham, three eggs, and a pot of coffee. It was a good night. These were the nights Holiday lived for, nights when the hunt narrowed in.

After dinner, he'd do some more draws, relax, rest up one more day, then head out along the Yellowstone River. To Jubal's way of thinking, Slade could only be headed one place . . . the new mining town called Silver Creek.

Chapter Fourteen

Denise lay in silence. Slade reached over and pulled a cheroot from his riggings. He fired it and puffed.

Denise scratched his arm playfully. "Thanks, Slade."

Slade couldn't remember a woman ever thanking him after a good romp. He turned to her. "But you're here to make a deal, right?"

"No one told me to come."

Slade chuckled. "But you did, right?"

Denise caught his pun. She laughed and slugged him playfully in the belly. "Yeah, I did, and I ain't never felt that good before, Slade, but then I got no reference in this kind of play.

"Don't give me that," Slade said, "I'll bet you go through men like—"

"No, no," she interrupted.

Slade let it be. "But you wanted to talk to me?"

"Yes," Denise sighed. She got up, swung over to the side of the bed, and pulled her skirt down. "I've come to persuade you to help us. My pa's sick, Mr. Slade. He'd dying of consumption. He knows it, I know it, but my ma doesn't. If we don't make some money off the mines Dad will die broke, and Mom and I will be left with nothin'."

Slade pulled her back across his legs, lifted up off the pillow, and bent over. He kissed her tenderly. "I'm sorry to—"

"I've done all my cryin' and frettin' about it, Slade. Now, I'm thinkin' about my ma. She's not a very forceful woman. We coulda been rich already, at least had enough money to see us comfortable for a few years, if it hadn't been for Brady."

Denise sat back up, turned, and faced Slade. He lay back, threaded his fingers behind his head.

"It's this apex law," Denise said. "The miners formed an association to fight Brady, but the men are miners, not gunfighters like you. All of us came here as prospectors. We found gold. Lots of it. And it was easy at first, but it played out quickly. We had to move on or consider hard-rock mining."

Slade got up, found his Durham, and rolled a cigarette. He lay back down and smoked. "Hard-rock mining attracts men with different inclinations and abilities than placer mining." he said.

"You're right about that, Slade. Hard-rock mines are different, especially for the miners out in Crooked Gulch. Most were in Deadwood, most mined the streams. Anyway, it took a long time to dig down to paying ore. Once that was found a mill had to be built . . . gimme that cigarette, I'd like a pull."

Again, Denise surprised Slade. "You're too young to smoke," he said.

Denise reached down and lifted the roll of tobacco from Slade's hand, took a deep drag, inhaled, and blew a thin puff from the corner of her mouth. She handed it back to Slade.

"Anyway," Denise continued, "we had to build a mill, and that's another reason the men formed the miners' association. They needed machinery. So, all the money we'd made mining Silver Creek went into that."

Slade got back up. He could see this was going to be a long chat. He found his whiskey and went to the chiffonier. He poured himself a good, strong shot into a thick glass. "I suppose you want a drink of whiskey, too," he said.

"Yeah, I'd like a little slug," Denise said. She lifted one leg over the other, her black boots shining in the dappled moonlight that splashed through the hotel window.

Slade poured her one. He was beginning to like Denise. He felt comfortable around her. No doubt about it. She was beautiful. She had a slim, fine body, and the way she carried herself reminded Slade of Charlotte Adams back in Deadwood.

Slade handed Denise the glass. She swilled it around in her hand, brought it up to her nose, sniffed it, then tossed the shot down.

"I wouldn't mind another," she said, handing the glass back to Slade.

Slade walked back to the chiffonier.

"How old are you?" he asked.

"I told you before, I'm old enough," she snapped.

Slade handed her another drink. Denise took the glass

and this time sipped slowly. Slade sat down in the chair beside the dresser. He tipped his own drink and chugged it down.

"Now where was I?" Denise asked.

"The miners used their creek holdings to buy machinery to mine the hills."

"Oh, yes. And we staked claims all up and down Crooked Gulch. There were quartz ledges running for miles with an eighth to one half of pure gold."

Denise took another drink from her glass and looked over at Slade. "You look good sittin' over there like that, Slade." She smiled.

"I can return the compliment, Miz Rafferty. You look awful good too."

"Well, we thought we were all gonna be rich, very rich, Slade."

Slade struck a lucifer on the side of the chiffonier and fired up another cheroot. "And then along came Brady?"

"Yes. Brady and a man named Pringle. See, this Pringle was from the East. He holds a degree in geology from Brooklyn Poytechnic Institute. Well, shit, he knows all about underground mining. Course, we didn't know that at first."

Denise paused and finished her drink. She held the glass in one hand, rolling the bottom on the bed.

"How did he get out here?" Slade asked.

"Brady hired him. He came here when we opened the Lucky Chance, our big strike, and took a job as a miner. Gave him the opportunity to explore the whole valley. He must have made maps . . ."

"And then came the apex law?"

"You're ahead of me, Slade, but yes. He left the Lucky Chance and went to work for Brady. Course they had all that planned, the way we see it. But sure, then came the apex law."

"Which is?"

"It comes from California. They always seem to have a nudge on everybody out there. The law was designed to give every man an equal chance at the gold. See, the thing is, you have to satisfy the working requirements to hold a claim. And this law was sanctioned by the U.S. Congress back in 1870, but not many mining camps ever knew about it . . . that's how those men took over the mines down in Deadwood."

Slade got up, poured another drink for himself.

"You could replenish mine if you were a gentlemen," Denise said.

Slade smiled. "Why, of course, Denise."

He took her glass, splashed in a generous slosh of whiskey, and handed it back. She swilled it in circular motions in front of her crossed legs, then wetted her lips.

"The deal is that ownership of the surface part of a vein, or apex, gives the miner the right to follw that vein, together with all its dips, spurs, angles, and variations, as deep and as far as it leads him, even if it takes him beneath another man's claim."

"That's where Brady came in?"

Slade sat down again in the chair.

"Right," Denise said. "Brady had this man Pringle follow out the veins. Then they staked a claim and showed the recorder maps how their vein went under ours.

"What that means is, whoever owns the location where the mineral vein apexes or comes to the surface can follow that vein and mine it, even if it leads into the richest ore bodies of the neighboring mines. Brady bought up all the claims surrounding the Lucky Chance. He paid big money to some of the miners to sell out, and his veins led smack into the main Lucky Chance vein. Now he owns the mine.''

''And you're—''

''Yes, we were suddenly working for him. For Brady.''

''But this is a law. Can't the miners lawyer this in court?'' Slade asked.

''Sure we can, but Brady's got a trained geologist, and all the veins he apexes work out to his favor. And besides, the lawyers seem to want to keep up the dissensions, especially in mining claims, so they can make money off the folks fightin' over it. Lawyers can be shitty, Slade,'' Denise said, then tipped her glass and swilled down all the whiskey.

Slade had to smile again. ''You're right about that, young lady. And so can bankers.''

''Both work against the small people.''

Slade wanted to tell her the story of how Cliff Langdon, the Dodge City banker, killed his parents and stole their land, but he puffed his cheroot instead.

''And this Pringle, he could make a living just testifyin' in court for one side or the other, but since he's on Brady's payroll he testifies that way. It's not much different, Slade, than that new defense some killers have used based on the fact they were insane when they killed a man. It's all bewilderin' to the juries out here who decide the case. And even if it wasn't confusing to them, Brady owns the judge and buys the juries. There's no way for us to win.''

"Real slick deal for Brady." Slade said.

"Oh, hell, it's a beautiful deal for him. He gets Pringle to study claim maps once they're filed with the recorder's office, picks himself out a a small piece of unclaimed land, sometimes no more than a few feet square, picks it out between two good working mines, then records his claim and sits back and waits until we start infringing on his vein."

"Sounds like it's all legal," Slade said.

Denise finished her third drink. "Well, it is, but it isn't. Do you see what I mean? Those pearly-heads in Washington don't know what they done enacting a law like this."

So, every time you hard-rock a new vein, he ends up with the strike?"

"Exactly."

Slade took a deep breath. Now he knew why the syndicates ultimately ended up with all the good mines in Deadwood Gulch.

"I feel kinda dumb I never knew about this," he said.

"Well, you shouldn't. I don't think many people know about it . . . but Brady does . . . and he's been using the law to . . . to . . . to . . . ."

Slade could see the young girl was about to break into tears. "To screw you," he said, without thinking.

Denise broke into sobs. "Yes! Yes! That's what's been takin' place. Nothin' we do helps. He's got the mining engineer, the geologist, gunmen, killers—everything."

Her body shook. "That's why we need someone like you, Slade," she bawled. "Harper was Brady's best man, his enforcer. No one ever challenged him, then you simply walked up and killed him.

"No one's ever done something like that here in Silver

Creek. That's why the men were impressed, that's why I'm impressed. You can help us if you want to, if you will, Slade.

Slade got up, put his glass on the chiffonier, walked to Denise, lifted her glass, dropped it to the floor, and pushed her back on the bed. He lifted her and hiked her skirt.

He stretched out beside her and kissed her. Denise's arms wrapped around him and pulled him down on top of her.

He fingered into her thick brown hair and laid her head gently on the pillow. Denise opened her legs.

"Do me again, Slade," she whispered.

Slade slid his hands under Denise and cupped her beautiful ass. She reached out and pulled him down, put him in.

"Does this mean you'll work with us, Slade, you'll help us?" Denise whispered.

She seemed a little too anxious to get Slade's word. He wondered if there wasn't another angle. He rocked slowly on her and said, "Give me a couple days."

Denise pushed up to him. "The association will pay you well, Slade."

She locked him in, her legs crisscrossing behind Slade. He looked down into her pretty face, the country-girl freshness.

"I'll think on it," Slade said.

Denise smiled. "But right now you're too busy thinkin' on me, huh?"

Slade bucked harder. Denise's smile changed. She bit her lower lip. It wasn't so much a smile as it was an expression, the way you corkscrew your face after sucking on a ripe lemon.

"Yeah, yeah, Slade," she urged. "Like that. Like that!"

Just before Slade took her, he wondered whether Denise had come to see him on her own or had been sent by the miners . . . or someone else.

But he'd have time to figure that out. Right now the young lady was offering herself to him with that excited, passionate look etched upon her face.

Chapter Fifteen

Slade left the Wheeler House dressed in the black suit he'd purchased in Miles City. He threaded his way through the crowds of miners on the sidewalk and made his way to the Golden Nugget Saloon and Gambling Hall.

He slipped through the bat-wing doors and ambled up to the bar. The smoke was thick. He ordered a bottle of Sweet Home and a shot glass, poured one, knocked it back, and turned to survey the surroundings.

A white-haired fellow hawked a gaming table. "Come on up, boys, put your money down. Money's as easy as the gold and silver you find in the gulch. Come on up. Everybody beats the old man. The girls even beat the old man. The old fool. Come on up and put your money down. Put some money down and be a winner."

Older women worked the tables as dealers. Slade checked them out. They had unscrupulous hands and used their female subtlety in various cheating devices.

Slade didn't see any faro, a game at which a dealer has practically no percentage if honestly played.

Miners, cowboys, and drifters filled the gambling hall. Slade took his bottle and walked through the throng to a table in the adjoining café. He ordered a T-bone and lit a cigar, then sat back sipping and thinking about the events of the day.

A tall, thin man, finely dressed, approached his table. "You the fellow called Slade?"

"Who's askin'?"

"Abel Brady, Mr. Slade. I own this saloon. May I join you for a drink?"

"Suit yourself."

Brady sat down. "That's a fine bottle of whiskey you have there. Let me buy your dinner."

Slade nodded.

Brady summoned a waitress and instructed her to put Slade's evening on the house. Then he leaned across the table. His face was pocked, pitted, and he scratched at his cheek. "I hear you're fast with a pistol, Mr. Slade."

Slade held his silence.

"You killed my best man."

"Harper?"

Brady nodded. "I hear you had a disagreement with him over a young lady."

"I think you're mistaken. Your man was pressuring some miners."

"That would be the group who formed the association. They're a nuisance."

Slade poured a shot and eyed Brady. The man had a square-cut face. He wore a blue suit, with expensive rings on both hands, and he continued pawing his pitted face.

"Get to the point," Slade said.

"This is a growing town, Slade. Booming, as they say. Full of wild men and women, men who spend their money on liquor, women, gambling. There are many opportunities here in Silver Creek, especially for a man with a fast gun."

Slade finished his drink. "So?"

"I could use someone like you in my operations."

"In what way?"

"You could have Harper's old job. Kind of protect my interests, the Brady Mining Company, this saloon, and my finest establishment, the Regal Hotel."

Slade wondered if the Regal was where Brady kept the young women Carlson had told him about back in Miles City.

"The Regal is the best place in town. Fine bar, exquisite dining room, gambling, and some of the finest and prettiest young women available you've ever seen. You could work there."

"How much would you pay?" Slade asked.

"Two hundred a week."

"Not enough."

"Three hundred."

"I'll think about it."

"You got a record, Slade?"

"Would that make a difference?"

"Might and it might not. I'm not anxious to have the law around."

"I thought you controlled the law in this town," Slade said.

"That's true, but that doesn't stop the federal marshals working these days."

"I'm always interested in money," Slade said.

"Then you'll take my offer?"

"I'll consider it."

"Look, this is a wild town, full of young punks who think they're hot with the draw. They cause trouble. Then I get the drunk miners—"

"And you need someone who can take care of them," Slade interrupted.

'You took Harper down. He was the fastest on the draw I ever saw. He was my man. I need a replacement."

"The miners might make me a better offer."

"I wouldn't take it if I were you, Slade."

"You're not me, though."

Brady smiled. "I like your brashness. Let's make it three-fifty a week."

"Give me a day or two. I'll let you know," Slade said.

Brady got up. "Fine, good. You'll find me at my office in the Regal Hotel. Come see me."

The waitress brought Slade's steak. Brady looked down at Slade, scratched at his cheek, and said, "I own this town, Slade. I own most of the mines out in the gulch. I'm going to own this whole part of Montana someday. You can be part of it. You'll end up a rich man."

Brady turned and left. Slade cut into his steak, chewed it, washed it down with a sip of whiskey, and thought things over.

Carlson and his daughter, the young girl Denise, the miners, Brady . . . lots to think about. But the most important thing on Slade's mind was Jubal Holiday. He wondered just how long it would take Holiday to show up in Silver Creek.

Chapter Sixteen

Slade finished dinner and returned to the Wheeler House. His body cried for rest. He stripped down, poured a tin basin full of water from the pitcher on the chiffonier, and washed.

He slid into bed with his Colt .45 and slept lightly, waking with a jolt at the slightest noise in the hall. He had to stay alert. Holiday could roll into town at any moment. And besides, he had no idea how serious Brady was about hiring him. Maybe Brady would prefer him dead.

The next morning Slade slept late, got up, and went to the small dining room in the Wheeler House. He ordered a ham steak, four eggs, a pot of coffee, and hot potatoes.

He spent the afternoon reading up on the apex law at the recorder's office. Denise had been right. The law was on the books, and it did give a man the right to apex a vein on another man's claim.

He went back to the Wheeler House and napped for a short time, then dressed for the evening in his black suit, white shirt, and black Stetson. He'd decided to play along with Brady. It was the only way to find out if Calla Carlson was being held by him, and that was why he was in Silver Creek in the first place.

The sun hung in an orange ball over the top of a far hill as Slade pushed through the noisy crowd on the board sidewalks.

Silver Creek wasn't much different from the way Slade remembered Deadwood the previous year, both springing up along gulches rich in gold and silver. Deadwood's heritage would be gold, and Silver Creek would be known for silver.

The parlor house girls posed lewdly on the porches. One older woman sat on a railing as if she were riding a horse sidesaddle, her bright red skirt hiked up above her knees. She curled a finger at Slade and smiled.

Silver Creek, the stream, ran behind the main street, up against a hill. As Slade passed an alley he looked down at the rushing creek and saw an abandoned sluice rig.

News of the strike in Silver Creek had brought a rush of men over from Virginia City. Burros and pack horses, loaded with outfits, lined the main street.

There wasn't much left to mine around Virginia City or Bannack, both just a few miles to the southwest of Silver Creek. Any news of a strike sent prospectors and drifters scurrying.

Slade had read in *Harper's Weekly* that Virginia City,

at the height of its glory days, bustled with a population of 12,000.

The hills in southwest Montana were filled with men looking for a new strike, and now they were crowding into Silver Creek.

Just like Deadwood the year before—when a trio of shrewd Californians, George Hearst, James Ben Ali Haggin, and Lloyd Tevis, had taken over the big strike in Lead, just four miles southeast of Deadwood, and set up the Homestake Mining Company—Brady was now establishing himself in the Tobacco Root Mountains.

Slade walked by a café featuring French coffee, a Chinese restaurant, a new bank, an opera house, two saloons, and then passed another side street on which homes had been built that featured signs on the lawns offering rooms to boarders.

The Regal Hotel, Saloon, and Casino was a huge two-story affair. Slade walked into the plush lobby, past potted palms, a checkout counter, and a reading corner, and then into the saloon and casino. He made his way to a thick, expensive bar that looked as though it had been chipped and sculptured by design. Instead of the usual wooden shelf of whiskey, Slade was surprised to find oak library shelves stacked with the best domestic and imported liquors.

A tall bartender smiled. He was dressed in a white shirt with ruffles, black string tie, and a long red apron. "What'll it be?" he asked.

Slade took a while to inspect the shelves. "Pour me a shot of Yukon Pleasure."

The apron set a thick shot glass in front of Slade and filled it to the rim. Slade reached into his pocket to pay.

"That's on me, Bill."

It was Brady. He stood behind Slade scratching his pockmarks, smiling. "I see you decided to accept my invitation, Mr. Slade."

Slade sipped the whiskey. "Mmm,mmm."

"Well, you see I have quite an enterprise here, only the finest whiskey, fine furnishings. This bar, for example—had it done by the people at Bannack Lumber. A work of art. Brand new expensive felt on the gaming tables, just look around, and a velvet curtain for the stage—"

"And lots of beautiful young women," Slade added.

"Ah, you noticed. The very best, Slade, and as you can see, all outfitted in fashions direct from San Francisco. The miners find the girls attractive. They like to come here after they've had a prosperous day working the streams."

It was obvious the girls shilled for Brady, got the miners to spend all their gold and silver. Slade gazed carefully at the young women. They looked out of place in their rich clothes, but they were intriguing, beautiful. Some wore pointed necklines with lavishly trimmed collars, others were dressed in gorgeous promenade dresses with corded silk. One girl had on a two-color bustle gown with fringe and accordion pleating in the front. All the girls wore expensive gloves, and most of them swished fans in front of their pretty faces.

Slade saw two women with parasols over their shoulders that had silk linings and lace outer coverings. A girl who hustled the poker tables wore a bustle dress with the hem and sleeves trimmed in tight frills.

"Notice that my women don't wear the usual saloon attire. I have a fashion consultant who visits from the East. You'll see the brunettes in yellow, makes the skin paler and clearer, more vulnerable. The darker-complected girls wear red. The blondes are enlivened by the blue and orange. And always the tight-fitting tops, some plunging necklines. I like my girls to look proper but alluring, as if they are out for a walk just after church. Drives these randy miners wild.''

Calla Carlson was the blonde in the orange dress and white gloves. She had her hair combed back and tied with a white ribbon at the nape of the neck. She was talking to a man at the far end of the bar.

Slade glanced away so he wouldn't draw suspicion. ''They all appear very young,'' he commented.

''They *are* very young, Slade. See anything you like? Take your pick. Say you'll work for me and you get your pick of the girls. We'll call it a bonus.''

''All beautiful, too.''

''Indeed.'' Brady smiled. ''Beautiful and in constant demand by the miners. The boys have nowhere else to spend their gold and silver. If they don't lose it at the gaming tables, they spend it on my young ladies. Either way, I win. How can you not join me, Slade?''

Slade smiled. ''Perfect setup.''

''See one you'd like to meet? You could go up to her suite. All my girls live in suites upstairs. No cribs in the Regal. They have their own little apartments where they live and work. Only the best, of course.''

''The brunette in yellow looks good,'' Slade said.

''That would be Miss Anne. Lovely, isn't she? Came here from Denver. Shall I speak to her for you?''

Slade nodded at Calla Carlson. ''Maybe that blond down the bar.''

''Oh, yes. An excellent choice, Slade. That's April.

She's from the East. Very refined. Educated. Went to a fine eastern college. Shall I call her over for a drink?''

Slade turned the proposal over in his mind. He didn't want to appear too anxious. He'd found Calla, that was the main thing. "Maybe later. I think I'll turn in early."

"Tomorrow perhaps?"

"Yeah, maybe tomorrow."

"Whatever you say, Slade, but think about my offer. I sure don't need a man like you working with the miners. I can use you here to manage the decorum at the Regal, keep peace among the rowdies when they've had too much to drink, or when they've lost all their money and become belligerent."

"I'm interested," Slade said, finishing his drink.

"Fine, because any man who drops Nick Harper can be on my payroll. We'll talk tomorrow?"

"I'm studyin' on it."

Brady leaned close. "Listen, my friend, you'll do much better with me than that gang of peasants out in Crooked Gulch."

Slade left the Regal and walked slowly around to the side of the hotel. It was on the corner of the block, constructed of sturdy lumber. He saw two men who appeared to be guards at each end of the hotel. They eyed Slade as he walked by. He came to the alley behind the Regal and turned. He looked up and saw lights from the girls' suites on the second floor.

Slade started down the alley.

"Hold it! No one allowed back here!" a man yelled, walking toward Slade, his shotgun leveled.

"Thought maybe I could take a shortcut through the alley."

"No way, mister. No one back here."

"Sorry," Slade mumbled.

He turned and walked back along the side of the hotel and saloon. Again he glanced up at the girls' suites. Brady had the women well guarded. It would be tough getting Calla Carlson out, if indeed she wanted to be freed.

Silver Creek was alive. Men gathered on the steps of cheap parlor houses bargaining with the whores. Drunken miners staggered from saloon to saloon. But it was apparent the main action was in Brady's establishments, the Nugget and the Regal.

Slade went back to his room at the Wheeler House. He stripped down to his balbriggans and opened the window to let in some fresh air. The sounds of the street below flooded his room.

He lay down on the bed and thought about Calla, her incredible beauty, her youthful appearance. Was she being held captive, forced into prostitution by Brady, or was she in Silver Creek on her own?

Chapter Seventeen

Slade went to the livery stable early the next morning and saddled his horse. He rode north out of Silver Creek and followed the stream toward Crooked Gulch. He found a trail that cut through the thick ponderosa pine until the terrain lifted into rugged mesas and mountains. He rode along the top of the rock formations and came back down to the creek.

He turned over the facts filed in his mind. He had a job to do for Carlson, to get his daughter back. But he also wanted to help the miners, help Denise.

Slade galloped alongside the whirling creek as it rushed down into Crooked Gulch. The creek bed led him into the mining camp.

It looked as though they had started with simple placer operations. Like 1849 all over again . . . pans, rockers, sluice rigs, picks, and shovels lay around the stream.

Slade trotted his horse past wagons loaded with heavy

equipment for the stamp mills. The men looked like professional miners, strong men of Irish or Cornish stock—mechanics and equipment operators.

Two mills were in operation crushing quartz that had been mined from the hills around the Gulch. The miners had elected to use the Colorado mill. It was lighter, cheaper, and required less horsepower. Not as good as the California mill, which could crush more ore than the slower stamp of the Colorado mill. It appeared the Crooked Gulch miners were excavating ore through open cuts in the hillsides, much like the Homestake in the Black Hills when it first started last year. But as Slade rode on he saw the shafts and square-set timbering that had been used in the Comstock strikes.

"Slade!"

It was Caleb.

"We've been waiting to hear from you."

Slade dismounted and shook Caleb's hand. He saw Denise approaching, young, sexy, in a burlap skirt, a slick black blouse, and black riding boots.

She smiled and walked up. "Mom has some coffee and breakfast cookin'."

She looked good to Slade—that square-cut face, the cheeks, her green eyes, the confident way she walked.

Caleb and Denise led Slade to a weathered shack of fir and logs that had been placed around a rude framework chinked with clay.

Mary, Caleb's wife, was at a huge iron stove cooking a rasher of bacon. She turned and nodded at Slade. Caleb pointed to a long wooden table in the middle of the room. Slade took a chair across from Denise. Mary served up a hearty plate of bacon, potatoes with gravy, and a steaming pot of black coffee.

Denise smiled and eyed Slade.

"Much obliged for the breakfast," Slade said.

"You come out to talk with us about our offer?" Caleb asked.

Slade nodded.

"We have a problem, Slade."

"The apex law?"

"Yes. Every time we go down, find a new vein—and I'll tell you, Slade, these hills around here are rich with silver—anyway, we go down, find a vein, then lose it to Brady."

"I know about the law. I studied it at the recorder's office."

"So, you know then, you know how it ends up. We get a little. Brady gets a lot."

"I understand."

"He sends out this little weasel, Sid Pringle. He's got a mining degree, knows geology, and because he defrauded us by workin' as a miner, he knows the whole area. He mapped out everything."

Slade looked at Denise. It was her story. But Slade listened to Caleb retell the miners' problems as he enjoyed breakfast.

When Caleb had finished Slade said, "But it's all legal."

"I guess it is, but that doesn't change the fact that he stole some of our claims earlier, some claims we marked along the creek."

"And what would you have me do about all this, sir?" Slade asked.

"Find a way to stop Brady."

Slade finished the potatoes and gravy, took the last

bite of eggs, and sipped coffee. He looked at Denise. She smiled coyly.

He pulled a freshly wrapped cigar from his pocket. "Mind if I light up?"

"No, not at all," Mary said.

Slade lit a lucifer on his thumbnail and fired the cigar. "Don't know how I can help."

"Well, can you consider it? We'd pay well. The association has some money. We pooled our resources. That's how we bought our equipment."

Slade was afraid Caleb was going to launch into another dialogue that he'd already heard from Denise. He interrupted him. "Give me some time to think about it."

"We'd pay you a thousand dollars."

"If I were to work for you it would be more expensive than that."

"I've been authorized by the association to go up to three thousand. That's the most we can pay, Slade."

Slade stood up. "I'll think on your offer, sir."

Denise followed Slade outside. He shook hands with Caleb and bid Mary good-bye, then turned to Denise.

She gave Slade a wicked wink.

Chapter Eighteen

Slade rode back to Silver Creek, quartered his horse, and walked to the Regal Hotel. It was late afternoon, and the place was filling.

He went to the end of the bar and ordered a shot.

"Brady here?" he asked the bartender.

"In his office in back."

"Send word Frank Slade wants to see him."

The bartender poured Slade a shot, then walked to the other end of the bar and whispered to a young gunman. The youngster disappeared into a hallway. A minute later Brady came out, looked around, saw Slade, and started for him.

"Come back to my office," Brady said.

Slade followed him across the saloon, down the hallway, and into a plush office that was much like Carlson's setup back in Miles City. Living quarters adjoining the office and both were richly appointed.

Brady sat down behind the desk and Slade took a chair in front.

"What'd the miners allow?" Brady smiled.

"Offered me a job."

"Mmm, mmm. And?"

"I thought it was a good offer," Slade said.

"What'd they want?"

"You."

Brady chuckled. "I use a legal law. It's—"

"The apex law," Slade said.

"Right."

"But before that, before you hired the mining expert from New York, the association said you stole their claims, killed a lot of men."

Brady smiled. "Do I look like a violent man, Slade?"

"Not at all," Slade said.

"I'm afraid the poor miners and their socialistic co-operative are doomed."

"Appears so," Slade answered.

"I don't worry much about 'em anymore."

"I suppose I wouldn't either if I had the apex law on my side."

"I expect they'll change that law one day, but for now I let it work for me."

A knock came on the door, it opened, and a man walked in.

"Sid, this is Frank Slade. He's handy with a six-shooter, and I been tryin' to hire him to keep a little order in the saloon and casino. Slade, meet Sid Pringle."

Slade appraised Pringle. He was a short, squat man with a big, muscular neck that rivaled his head in size and thickness. He had a hooked nose and fierce black eyes, and his face was solemn.

"I need to discuss some business. Will you be long?" Pringle asked. He nodded at Slade.

"Give me a few minutes with Mr. Slade."

Pringle left and Brady turned his attention back to Frank. "Well, what'll it be?"

"Let's talk money."

"A thousand dollar bonus and three hundred a week."

"And the other bonus?" Slade smiled.

"Oh yes. Of course, one of the girls."

"I'd like the blonde, I think her name was . . ."

"April, yes, yes, a fine young lady, Slade. Excellent choice. Come back after supper. I'll have it arranged. And after you've spent some time with the girl you can start work."

Slade got up.

"One more thing, Slade."

"Yeah?"

"You killed the best gunman I've ever hired. Harper kept things orderly here at the Regal. I expect you to do as good a job, maybe better, seein' you killed him."

Brady rose from his chair and went to a small safe in the corner of his office. He counted out a thousand dollars in gold and handed it to Slade.

Frank walked to his room at the Wheeler House, took a bath, and dressed in the new outfit he'd purchased in Miles City—all black with the white shirt. He added a black string tie, then strapped on his swivel rig and slipped a nitrate cap into his shirt pocket. He tried the gun. It swirled up easily from the soldered slot on the gun belt.

Slade looked dangerous, handsome, as he walked back to the Regal and pushed into the casino area. Brady stood near a poker table. He saw Slade and strode toward him with a smile.

Slade slipped out of his black coat. "I'll need to hang this," he said. "I can't work with it on."

Brady saw the swivel rig. "What the hell is that contraption, Slade?"

"Had it made special for me in Rapid City, over in Dakota Territory."

"No holster?"

"Right. Faster that way. The gun is soldered to a plate on the gun belt. Eliminates drawing out of the holster. Saves time. All I have to do is grip the handle and swivel it up."

"Good God, that's quite a deal, Slade."

Brady took Slade's coat. "I'll hang it in the hall by my office. April is waiting for you at the bar. You can go to her suite, spend as much time as you like, then start work."

Slade walked to the young blonde. She was fashionably attire in a long orange evening gown with fringe on the hem that swirled at the floor. She wore black gloves slipped skin-tight up to her elbows. A black pillbox hat sat on top of her blond hair, which fell in beautiful curls on her shoulders. Her bodice was tight and featured a décolleté neckline that lifted her young breasts in a salacious squiggle.

Calla smiled at Slade. Her lips were pink, glossy, glistening. Her cheeks had been rouged with a wine red blush. Her teeth were white, straight, and she had icy blue eyes.

"I'm Frank Slade."

"Yes, I know. I saw you the other evening in here. Mr Brady said you'd be spending some time with me . . . as much time as you like."

"Well, only if you agree," Slade said.

"I agree. It's very seldom I have the opportunity to entertain a handsome man."

"Drink?" Slade asked.

"A glass of champagne, please."

"I don't want you to do this if you aren't being paid properly."

"Oh, Mr. Brady is very kind to us, especially on special occasions like this. I'm at your service, Mr. Slade."

Frank ordered drinks and Calla said, "I'm April. Would you like to retire to my living quarters?"

Slade nodded and followed Calla to the second floor. He passed two guards at the top of the stairs. They walked to the end of the hall, and Calla unlocked the door.

Brady hadn't lied. His women lived in lavish suites—plush carpet, velvet curtains, oak trimming, expensive furniture, a small bar in the corner, a couch, a beautiful handmade chair, and a dining area. Off the living quarters Slade saw a small kitchen, and on the other side of the room a draped curtain led to a bedroom.

"Fix yourself a drink, Slade," Calla said. "I'm changing clothes."

Slade went to the bar, poured a crystal glass with a generous splash of Belker's, and sat down on the bar stool. He drew a mental picture of the layout, the hall, stairs, the guards, the girls' suites.

Frank still had to devise a plan to free Calla, his original assignment from Carlson.

But it wouldn't be easy. There would be shooting, and Slade didn't want to involve the girls, maybe get some of them killed.

He gazed about the suite, calculating the dimensions, noticing the Hart Lock on the door.

Taking the guards in the hall would be dangerous. They would shoot to kill. No doubt those were their orders. Brady was protective when it came to "his" girls. Slade could expect resistance to any move he made.

He heard Calla humming in the bedroom, and listened to the whisp of clothes, the crackle of her petticoats, as she changed for him.

Slade sipped the bourbon and poured himself another. Life was picking up. He was making money again. And if he were successful in getting Calla Carlson back to Miles City, he'd have enough cash to buy some time, find a comfortable hideout, take a riverboat south.

Frank always dreamed of luxurious freedom, a life where he wasn't known, wasn't wanted, a place where he could start over.

"Come on in the bedroom, Slade." Calla called.

Slade got up, pulled the curtain aside, and walked into her sleeping quarters.

Calla stood nude in laced black boots, the black pillbox hat propped provocatively on her head. She turned slowly around and let Slade appreciate her body.

Her narrow waist sloped into supple hips. Her legs were tapered, trim. Her breasts jutted beautifully from her chest. Her face was angelic, the cheeks tight around superior bone structure, and her pink lips and blue eyes made Slade tremble.

A blond nest of wiry curls between her legs was shaded in an alluring copper tinge—thick, rich, inviting. On her right thigh, in back, was a blusish bruise, as though she'd been hit there.

"You're fabulous," Slade whispered.

He felt a twinge of guilt. He had not come to Silver Creek to bed down with Carlson's daughter. He'd come to save her and take her back to her father in Miles City.

Calla smiled, sat down on the bed, patted it with her hand, and said, "Come sit with me."

Slade placed his glass of bourbon on the chiffonier and walked to the big four-poster bed. He sat down. Calla moved in close. She looked up into Frank's rugged handsomeness, his green eyes.

"Better take the gun off," she said, unbuckling Slade's swivel rig. She laid it on the floor.

"You couldn't be much older than me," Calla whispered.

"And how old would you be?"

"Twenty-three, Mr. Slade."

She reached down and slowly unbuttoned Slade's black pants. Her hand brushed the puffing erection that punched up against the serge.

Calla tugged Frank's pants down to his knees, then yanked his balbriggans down. His cock slapped up in a wild wobble.

"Mmm!" she said, sucking in her breath.

Calla's fingers curled around Slade's towering hard-on. She squeezed and bent over, her lips puckering as she touched him.

He pulled her up, off him, and removed her hand. "Let's talk," he whispered.

Calla turned and gave Slade an astonished, surprised look. "Talk?"

"Yes."

"Mr. Slade, I've had some strange requests since I started working here at the Regal, but that is just about the—"

"Not what you expected, right?" Slade said.

Calla's eyes glanced down at Slade's erection. "What about that?" she asked.

"It can wait," Slade said.

"Doesn't look like the waitin' kind," Calla purred, still staring at Slade's hardness. "You better let me pleasure it down."

Her fingers snuck over his thigh, and she grabbed his erection again. "We better take care of this thing before we talk, Mr Slade."

Calla seemed eager. Slade wanted to discuss her situation with her. "I'd rather talk first," he said.

He grabbed her wrist, twisted it until Calla released his thick cock.

Calla got up, lifted a silk robe from a nearby chair, and slipped into it. She came back to the bed. Slade pulled his clothes back up.

"Are you sure, Mr. Slade? Mr. Brady had paid me well to entertain you. I think he likes you."

A tension passed into silence, then Slade said, "You sure this is the kind of place you want to be?"

Calla flashed Slade a puzzled look. "I don't know what you mean."

"Do you want to go home . . . home to Miles City?" he said.

"What in the world are you talking about, Mr. Slade? My name is April. I would have no reason to go to Miles City. I've never been there."

Slade had played his card. He'd come to Silver Creek to find Calla, and now that he had, he needed to know if she wanted to return to Miles City. He had to take the chance she might tell Brady about his questions.

"I was passin' through Miles City on my way out here. I met a man who was lookin' for his daughter, said she might be here in Silver Creek. You look like her. The father is an old man. He wants his daughter back."

"If you're looking for this girl you're looking in the wrong place."

"You resembled her, that's all."

"Well, be that as it may, I'm April, and I intend to stay April."

Slade got up. "Sorry, guess I made a mistake."

"That's certainly obvious." April said.

Chapter Nineteen

Jubal Holiday was born on Christmas Day in Texas. His mother, an inventive, creative woman, christened him Jubal, for the jubilant time of the season.

Later, when his parents had died, Jubal changed his last name to Holiday. He like the sounds of it—*Jubal Holiday*. He thought it would read good in the legend he intended to write about himself with his fast gun.

He looked comfortable in the saddle as he rode along the Yellowstone, loose, relaxed, in rhythm with his horse, his weight into the stirrups.

The sun had dipped behind the tabletop mesas on the eastern edge of Bozeman, and dark clouds hung in the sky ahead. Jubal rode harder, faster. He wanted to make town before the storm hit.

A soft drizzle sprinkled his face as he galloped into Bozeman. He hooked his horse at the rail in front of the Bozeman Hotel and walked into the lobby.

Donna was sweeping behind the counter.

"Room?" she asked.

Jubal nodded. "And can you have someone quarter my horse at the livery stable?"

"Sure. It's fifty cents extra."

Jubal was tired, worn out from his long ride along the river. "I need a soft bed and some information," he said.

Donna pushed the register toward him. Jubal scanned it for Slade's name. Nothing.

Donna smiled. "What kind of information?"

"Any riders through here lately? Might be headed for the silver and gold strikes, maybe up to Butte for copper."

"Can't say as I remember anyone special. Always someone comin' through Bozeman, mister."

Holiday rolled a gold coin across the counter. "That's for the room." Then he spun another coin toward Donna. "Does that help your memory?"

Donna pocketed the coins. "Might help," she said.

"I'm lookin' for a man called Slade . . . tall, thin, good-lookin', black hair, rugged but young, got a square-cut face."

Holiday could tell by Donna's reaction he'd hit a responsive chord.

He reached into the top pocket of his lawman jacket and dropped his marshall's star on the counter. "Best you tell me the truth."

Donna fingered the badge. "Why would you be lookin' for this Slade?"

Holiday signed in. "He killed a man in Dodge City and robbed a bank."

"You look worn-out, real tuckered. I could bring some

hot water to your room for a wash, maybe a good bottle of bourbon. We could have a few drinks later when I get off work.''

Jubal gave Donna some more money. ''Sure, that sounds real good, especially the bourbon.'' He lifted his hat and brushed the blond curls from his forehead. ''Maybe you can refresh your memory while you're gettin' that bottle, huh?''

''Probably can,'' Donna said. ''You say his name was Slade?''

Holiday nodded.

''Would his first name be Frank?''

''That's him.''

''Sure, I'll refresh my memory about Frank Slade, see if I can remember him comin' through here, where he might have been headed. That what you want to know?''

Jubal smiled and took the room key she dangled.

He walked up the wooden stairs. The hunt was closing in. He liked that. Made him feel good.

Real good.

Chapter Twenty

"**T**his game is rigged!" the miner shouted. "I ain't lettin' Brady cheat me no more!"

Slade heard the commotion at the poker table. He sauntered over. The miner was standing up, a bear of a man with a thick beard.

"What's the problem here, friend?" Slade asked.

"The dealer. He's placin' the cards."

"Now, you made a mistake, mister," Slade said. "This is a clean game."

"I'll be damned if it is!" the miner shouted.

The piano player stopped. The other gamblers held up their games.

The miner reached for his gun, but before he could hit his holster, Slade had the swivel rig in action and his .45 pointed.

The miner's hand trembled over his holster. "I know you," he snarled at Slade. "You're the louse we tried to hire out at the mines. You oughta be whipped for tyin' in with Brady.''

''Let's go. Time to go home,'' Slade said.

''Bullshit on that! Not 'til I get my money back!''

He drew his gun and ran toward Brady's office in the back of the Regal. Slade took off after him, tackled him in the hallway. The miner sprawled forward, his gun clinking to the floor. He jumped back up. Slade smashed a hard right in his face. The miner went down.

''Get up and get goin' . . . get!'' Slade yelled.

The miner crawled to his hands and knees, then rose. He charged Slade. Frank hammered another punch, a roundhouse right. The big man sagged. Frank grabbed him and dragged him through the casino area to the lobby, then tossed the miner into the street.

Slade walked back into the crowd. Things returned to normal. Brady approached him. ''See? That's why I hired you, Slade. We can't have that here at the Regal, can't have some idiot like that making scurrilous charges against me. Good job.''

Slade nodded and walked to the bar.

Over the next week Slade worked the Regal and kept the plush hotel, saloon, and casino free of trouble. But he expected Jubal Holiday any day.

A strange thing was happening with Holiday up in Bozeman. He spent two days enjoying the talents of Donna, eating, drinking, resting up for his encounter with Slade. Then one night, slipping into bed, he had his first ever jolt of fear.

It was a feeling that shook Jubal so badly he decided to stay in Bozeman a few more days so he could deal with the problem. In all his years of gunfighting, trailing men, and fast draws, not once had he ever experienced fear.

Could he be getting too old?

Jubal worked hard out back of the hotel in a vacant lot, practicing his draws, shooting cans off fence posts, procrastinating—trying to break the cloud of fear that had formed over him like the black thunderheads in the sky the night he rode into Bozeman.

Holiday couldn't turn back. He had to go through with the plan. He could never live with himself if he quit a coward. He had to face Slade.

It could have been luck, it might have been fate, another spin of Fortuna's wheel, that young Johnny Wade showed up in Bozeman. He approached Jubal at the Bozeman Café. Holiday sat in the back slicing into a steak.

"Jubal Holiday?" Wade asked, walking confidently up to his table, new pearl-handled six-guns in a double rig strapped to his thin hips.

"Yeah?"

"I hear you're lookin' for Frank Slade?"

Jubal nodded.

"Then we got a problem, because I'm lookin' for him too, and I aim to get him."

Wade pulled a chair and sat down without invitation.

"So?" Jubal said.

"I want the reward."

"You figure you can take Frank Slade?" Jubal asked.

Wade jumped up. His guns were out so fast it stunned Holiday. Wade smiled boyishly. "See? Tell me I ain't gonna drop Frank Slade."

Holiday pushed his steak away. "Fast. That's real fast, kid."

"I hear you're no slouch either," the kid said. He holstered his guns and sat back down.

Holiday pulled a toothpick from his pocket and poked at his teeth. His eyes beaded in on young Johnny Wade.

"Eighteen, nineteen?" Jubal said, rolling the toothpick from one corner of his mouth to the other.

"Age ain't got nothin' to do with it."

"But you're out to make a name, right?"

"Like you did." Wade grinned. "I read all about you."

"And you want a draw with me. The winner gets Slade, is that it?"

Johnny Wade smiled. But Jubal's answer was implicit in the boy's grin.

A pang of fear sliced through Jubal, but he held himself strong. "You lose anyway you look at it, kid."

Wade's smile faded. "How's that?"

Jubal pulled open his vest. "I'm a federal marshal these days. Let's say, just for conversation, that you beat me on the draw. You could never take Slade back for the reward. They'd put you in prison for killin' a marshal. If you didn't beat me in a draw—which you'd never do, kid—you'd be dead. See? You lose."

The two gunfighters stared at each other across the table. The old, the young. Jubal held the best hand and Wade knew it.

"But I like your spunk, kid. You remind me of myself years ago. I been thinkin' about takin' on a deputy. You could go with me. You could learn some tricks from me. We could share the reward, work together."

Wade's eyebrows lifted, as did the fear that weighed upon Holiday. A young kid like Wade, fast as lightning on the draw, meant insurance. Two against one. Slade wouldn't have a chance.

"Well, I didn't know you'd been badged a marshal, and I ain't lookin' to kill one." Wade paused, gazed long and hard at Holiday. "You wanna take me on? You'll teach me some of the things you know? We'd share in the money?"

"Sure, why not?"

"Why would you do that? Doesn't sound like the Jubal Holiday I read about in the papers."

"Shit, kid, I'm a fair man. I'm an honest man. I tell the truth. Gets lonely workin' alone all the time. I could use a partner."

Wade was apprehensive.

"You could back me up. I like your spirit. I like your timing with those guns."

Johnny Wade stuck out his hand. "Got yourself a deputy, Mr. Holiday," Wade said. He was still puzzled by Holiday's offer, but he could figure things out as they went along. Might be Holiday was getting too old. Might be Jubal planned to kill him.

"Slade's in Silver Creek, right?" Wade asked.

Jubal nodded.

"He ain't got a chance against us," Johnny Wade said.

"Yeah, you remind me of myself, kid. I like you." Jubal smiled, but he knew deep down that after they had taken Slade and collected the reward, he would hang up his gun.

He'd have to. Sooner or later a kid like Wade would kill him, just as Jubal had done to an older shootist he'd ridden with in his early days.

But for now Johnny Wade was an asset.

Chapter Twenty-one

Sid Pringle sat in the back of the saloon poring over maps of Crooked Gulch. The miners had hit another rich vein, and Pringle found the intersect where it apexed with Brady's property.

Slade stood at the bar watching Calla. She had been distant since the night he visited with her. But there was one good thing. She had obviously not mentioned anything about his questions to Brady.

Slade turned and found the owner sliding in beside him at the bar. Brady dug his nails into his cheek. He was all business. "Sundays the girls go for a ride in the buckboard. They like to stop and walk near the creek. They need the fresh air and exercise. You'll go with them, along with a couple other men. You're not to let the girls out of your sight, is that clear?"

Slade ventured a loaded question. "Would they try to leave?"

"Of course not," Brady snapped. "But I have all these women under contract. You never know what they'll do . . . I mean, they'd never run away, but with money involved, oh, hell . . . just do as I say, Slade."

"Sure, Mr. Brady."

Six girls lived in the suites on the second floor of the Regal. Sunday morning Slade sat tall on his Appaloosa as the girls were helped by one of their guards into the buckboard. The driver headed down the creek into the gulch. Slade rode behind. Another guard trotted his horse in front.

The girls were fashionably dressed, even for the ride, and all of them seemed calm and assured. One of the girls waved back at Slade.

"We'd like to stop here and go for a walk, get some exercise."

Slade signaled to the driver to stop and got off his horse. He helped the girls from the buckboard, instructed the driver to keep a lookout, and told the other guard to walk in front of the girls while he brought up the rear.

He thought about how easy it might be to break the girls free right now. Kill the other guards. But then what? How far would they get in a buckboard?

No, he'd have to come up with a better plan.

The girls walked ahead of Slade, chatting, following a narrow path, walking two by two.

Slade thought it over. If the girls were not being held against their will, then why was he guarding them? He turned this question over in his mind. Then Calla Carlson dropped back of the other girls and joined Slade on the path.

"I'm taking a big chance telling you this, but I think I can trust you, Frank Slade."

Slade didn't say anything, just kept walking.

"Can I?"

"Try me."

"You were right. I am Calla Carlson."

"I knew that."

"I figured you did."

"Then why did you lie to me?" Slade asked.

"Brady tests us. He sends men to our suites on occasion who ask us questions like you did. If we tell the truth we take a beating."

"I see."

"Maybe not as well as you should. That girl up there in blue?"

"Yes."

"Last week she was tested, she made a mistake. Her legs are black and blue from a stick beating. She has to wear dark stockings to cover the bruises. And you saw the swelling on my thigh."

"So, you're being held against your will?"

"Yes."

"Were you kidnapped?"

"Walking down the street in Miles City one evening. They just lifted me up and carried me to a horse, tied me to it, drugged me, and the next thing I knew I was in Silver Creek."

"And you want to go home to Miles?"

"Oh, God yes."

"I was sent by your father," Slade whispered.

Calla took a deep breath, sighed heavily. "I knew he wouldn't let me down."

"Okay, go back up with the other girls. Let me figure

a way to get you free. It might take awhile. Meantime you continue on as if nothing has happened.''

"You'll get me out of here, get me back to Miles City?" Calla stuttered, tears forming in her eyes.

"Just give me some time."

"We're well guarded, Mr. Slade. I don't how one man can do it."

"That's my problem, Miss Carlson. You let me worry about it. I'll figure a way."

Calla walked forward to join the other girls, then stopped and turned to Slade. "About the other night. You understand I was doing what I had to do?"

"I understand that," Slade said.

She smiled. "Thanks . . . but I will say this . . . it's the first time I enjoyed being with a man since I was brought here."

Slade waved her back to the other girls.

The chips were falling into place. Brady had kidnapped the girls. A serious crime. Very serious. And Frank Slade aimed to make him pay for it.

Chapter Twenty-two

Slade took the girls back to the Regal and led them into the hotel. Brady was standing in the lobby. Slade pushed Calla.

"Get along, don't lag behind all the time."

Calla moved quickly across the lobby to the stairs, then went up to her room with the rest of the girls.

"That one give you some trouble, Slade?" Brady asked.

"Naw, nothin' I can't handle."

"She's stubborn. A looker, but stubborn. I thought that was the girl you spent some time with the other night. Didn't she treat you right?"

"Yeah, she was okay."

"I might have to have a little chat with April. She's given me trouble before."

Slade turned and started for the door. He was off for the rest of the day. He hated to put Calla in a bad position with Brady, risk having her beaten, but he had to keep his cover.

"Slade!" Brady called.

"Yeah?"

"Good job. I like the way you handle yourself around here."

"Thanks, Mr. Brady." Slade smiled.

He walked to the Wheeler House. He was eager to finish reading his *Harper's Weekly*, get some rest, and think about how he could free Calla.

He went to his room, unlocked the door, and found Denise sitting in the chair by the chiffonier. She wore a silky black skirt, black laced boots, and a red blouse. Her brown hair was tied in the back with a white ribbon.

"How did you get in here?" Slade asked.

Denise ignored his question. She stood up, walked briskly to Slade, and slapped his face with a wicked right. "You shitty jerk!" she huffed. "I thought you were gonna help us. I thought we had an understanding."

She raised her arm to crack him another good one. Slade reached out and caught her by the wrist.

"Now wait a minute, Denise."

"How could you go to work for Brady? I thought you were a better man than that."

"Don't jump to these all-fired conclusions. How do you know what I'm really up to? In fact, how do you know anything about me? You don't. So—"

"I know enough to hate you. You used me!"

"Used you? I could turn that around against you."

Denise tried to wrench her arm free. Slade held her tight, pulled her into his lean body. "Just cool down a little, Denise."

Her fine, lithe body felt good against Slade. She smelled fresh. Her hair had just been washed and she had a light rouge on her cheeks. She looked up into Slade's face. Her chin jutted out, her eyes full of emotion.

"How'd I know what you were up to the other night? I've learned to play my cards close. I don't trust anyone these days. Learned too many hard lessons."

Denise wiggled against him as she tried to pull free of his strong grip. Her anger seemed genuine, so Slade told her why he had come to Silver Creek. He related his story and felt Denise relax against him.

"I always thought maybe those girls weren't workin' in that hotel just for the profit of it. Good God, Slade. You mean Brady holds them like prisoners?"

"But you have to keep quiet about this, Denise, until I figure a way to handle things. If I can nail Brady on this kidnapping charge some way, then that would take care of the miner's problems too."

Denise's arms went around Slade's broad shoulders. She lifted her face. He kissed her. Her lips tasted sweet. His hands roamed her back, dipped down below her waist. She pushed against him. The warmth of her mouth sent a shudder through Slade's thin, wiry body.

Slade lifted her and lay her on the bed. Denise reclined in rippling luxury, her skirt up, her legs open, knees cocked.

"If you're lyin' to me, Frank Slade, I'll kill you," she whispered.

Slade smiled. "I believe you would, Denise."

"Take your clothes off, Slade."

He stripped down. Denise wore nothing under her skirt. Her thick brown softness invited Slade. He mounted her, slid an arm under her back, his other hand curled behind her rump. Denise reached up and clutched his wobbling hardness.

She pulled him down and Slade pushed in.

"Ah, awww, yeah . . . but not too fast now with that big thing, Slade," Denise whispered.

Slade pumped.

He kissed her mouth again and Denise opened her legs wider. Slade rocked up and down, punching deeper. There was a need within him that was demanding, urgent.

Denise broke the kiss. "That's enough. Right there. Don't shove anymore," she whispered.

Slade followed her instructions, but kept his stroke lean and tender, picked up speed, and thumped hard at Denise's wild bumping.

"Good, Slade! Good!" she cried.

"I know."

"Keep at it, keep me on the edge like this, Slade!"

Slade silenced her babbling with another kiss, then felt her quake under him. Her legs locked up and squeezed him in. She shuddered, pulled her mouth away from his kiss, and squealed, "Damn you, Slade! Damn you!"

Slade banged harder. Their bodies slapped at each other until he couldn't hold back any longer. Denise bucked him furiously, drained him completely.

She fell back on the bed, huffing, puffing, and Slade lay spent on top of her.

Denise sighed and asked. "You got any liquor, maybe some tobacco? I feel like a little drink."

Slade smiled to himself as he got up to fulfill Denise's request.

"I still think you're too young, but I guess I can fix ou a drink and roll one."

Denise rose on her side, propped her pretty face on ne hand, her elbow cocked into the bed, and watched lade pour her a splash of whiskey.

"If you're lyin' to me, Slade, I'll kill you, I really vill," Denise said.

Slade brought the glass to her. "I believe that, Denise. I believe you'd find a way to do that," he whispered.

Chapter Twenty-three

Jubal Holiday and Johnny Wade had made camp few hours out of Silver Creek. They sat around a early morning campfire.

Holiday had brought a jug of whiskey with them from Bozeman. He pulled the cork and took a long swig.

"You been drinkin' too much," Wade growled. "Yo said you'd show me a few things. You ain't done tha yet."

Jubal sighed. "I did make that deal with you, didn' I?" he said, and took another sip of whiskey. "Lemm see what you got, kid."

Johnny Wade jumped up, took a stance. "You lear to use both hands," he said, "use the left one, like do, and it gives you twice as good a chance."

Wade's hands blurred with smoking Colts. He sho little pieces of shale, blasted them off the top of boulder nearby.

"Pretty damn good," said Jubal.

"Most carry only one gun, like you." Johnny Wade smiled. "I carry two." He spun the guns, the right forking into his left hand, the left Colt twirling into his right. "I know how to use both hands. Gives me an edge."

"Ah, shit," Jubal said. "You got a lot to learn before we take on Slade."

"He ain't gonna be that tough. I heard about him. He ain't that fast."

"He's smart. That makes up for it."

"So what can you teach me, old man?" Wade smirked.

"You're concentratin' too much on your sights. Forget 'em, keep your arm half cocked."

"Like this?" Wade said, assuming a stance.

"Now drop the hammer."

"Ah, I see," Wade said, relaxing.

"Let's say you're facing two men. What do you do?" Jubal asked. "Show me."

"I take 'em with a two-gun draw."

"No, no, no," Jubal said. "Shoot the man on your left first. He's the hardest to hit."

"Ah, sure. Why didn't I think about that?" Wade said, shaking his head.

" 'Cause you're too damn busy being cute. You oughta learn to shut up and listen."

"I'm listenin'," the kid said.

"Shoot and hit while you're movin'. You been standin' there lookin' cute with your double draw, but you leave yourself a disadvantage. *Move!* You can kill the man who's got the bead on you if he's standin'. But you stand like that and a man rolling on the ground can kill you because he's tougher to hit. I thought you would have known this, Wade. It's elemental.''

"Well, I'm young," the kid said, then flashed his bright smile.

"Shootin' a man is different than shootin' shale off rocks," Jubal said.

"Tell me some more," Wade urged.

"Use a rifle if you can. It's faster and more accurate."

"Makes sense," Johnny Wade said, "What else?"

"Aww, shit, let's have a drink," Jubal said.

"I told you, Holiday, you're drinkin' too much. You'll lose your edge."

Jubal took another pull from the bottle, then stood up slowly. It was as if every piece of him moved into synchronization as he rose.

He had been drinking more than usual. The booze gave him the high he needed to put himself on the line against killers like Frank Slade.

It wasn't like that in the old days, when he first started, back when he was a kid like Johnny Wade. Then he never touched alcohol or anything that might impair his fast draw.

But lately he had to suck down a bottle of whiskey to get himself ready for a face-off. Once he'd oiled himself good enough, he was always ready, always fast, on target.

"Okay, what you really want is a draw with me," Jubal drawled. "That's what you want."

"I didn't say that."

"You talk about my drinkin', you make comments I don't like. You're too damn cute. I don't want you goin' up against Frank Slade with me."

"Now look, Holiday. I never did mean nothin'."

"Let's have a draw. I'll bet ten thousand I can take you."

"Ten thousand?" Wade gasped.

"Sure. You think I'm gonna kill a man for nothin'?" Jubal said, his mouth wrinkling into a confident smile.

"I ain't got that kind of money," Wade said.

"Than you got no business playin' this game. You're all talk. A liability. You don't even have the admission."

"Now stop," Wade snapped. "I ain't gonna let you talk to me like that."

"But I am."

Wade jiggled from one foot to the other. Jubal stood ready, his hand hooked out, his elbow cocked.

The old gunfighter. The brash kid. A face-off in the heat of early sun. Jubal waited. The kid stared at him.

"Awww, hell, you said you'd teach me. I ain't gonna draw with you. Not now."

Jubal sat down.

He put a pot of coffee over the fire. Wade sat down across from him.

"You're good, kid. You got moves. But you got lots to learn."

The fire crackled. Flames licked the gray coffeepot.

"I know I do," Wade said. "You said you'd teach me."

"I will, I will," Jubal mumbled.

Holiday felt his confidence returning. It was like a rushing stream flowing through his body. Then just as quickly it dried up. These mood swings bothered Jubal. One moment confident he would repeat his success, but the next moment doubting his ability to chalk up one more kill.

Wade, the kid, could only be considered an asset. Three guns were better than one.

"So, how did you get into this business anyway?" Wade asked.

"The killing business?"

"Yeah, how'd that happen?"

Jubal took the coffee off the fire, poured two cups full, handed one to Wade, then sat back and sized up the lad.

"I was like you, eighteen, maybe seventeen. I saw my daddy dancin' in the street while some gunmen pumped lead in a circle around his boots. I saw them make a fool of my father, watched them make him drink a fifth of booze. I was about twelve years old.

"I wanted to vomit. I couldn't believe that my own father was so weak, such a coward. Of course I later realized he had no choice, but I said to myself that I'd never let that same thing happen to me.

"So, I started practicin' with guns, even before my parents knew I had 'em. I shot tin cans off fence posts, I practiced fast draw, and by the time I was your age, Wade, I'd killed six men."

"You were hired?"

"After the first killing, when folks saw how fast I was . . . all that practice . . . I started getting offers from all over."

"I read about you, how you've killed over thirty men," Wade said.

"And that's what you want. You want the fame, the publicity. Don't you?"

Wade refused to answer. Just sat there and returned Jubal's cold stare.

"And now you want to be like me, right?" Jubal

whispered, his hands cradling a tin cup. He raised it to his lips, took a sip of coffee.

"We'll take Slade, right? Our deal's still on?"

Jubal set his cup on a rock, leaned forward, elbows on his knees. "We'll take Slade, no problem with that. We'll get our money. We'll get our publicity. You'll start your career as a gunfighter."

"Right. That's right. That's what we'll do," Wade agreed eagerly.

"Sure, we'll take Slade. That'll be easy. I get more excitement thinkin' about you and me after we take Slade, what will happen when we have it out."

"Hey, I wouldn't think of takin' you on, Mr. Holiday," Wade said.

"Yes, you will, after I teach you all I know. And I will, I'll give you every trick I've learned. I want to make us even in that respect, take it down to pure guts."

The two gunmen sat across the fire in silence. Wade looked at the ground, now and then glancing up at Jubal.

Finally Wade said, "Guess you're probably right about that, Holiday. Guess we will have to have it out one day, just for the record, huh?"

Jubal got up, spilled his coffee onto the ground, and looked at Wade.

"Sure we will, kid. Just for the record."

Chapter Twenty-four

Slade recognized Jubal Holiday immediately from Calamity Jane's description.

Holiday had regained his old confidence. Why not? He had Johnny Wade in the wings. Holiday was dressed in a pair of gray pants, black shirt, black Stetson, and black boots, and his gun belt was slung low on his right hip.

His tin badge looked ominous pinned to his shirt. His frizzy blond curls dipped just below the brim of his hat.

Frank watched him swagger toward him at the bar in the Regal. He dropped his arm, ready, waiting.

"Frank Slade?"

"You found him."

"I'm Jubal Holiday. I've come to take you back to Kansas to answer for murder and bank robbery." Heads turned at the mention of Holiday's name.

"Wrong! You've come to die," Slade growled.

"Oh, I don't think so, Slade."

"Cliff Langdon send you?"

The saloon and casino area had tapered off to a buzz of soft voices. Men, the girls, everybody eyed the encounter at the bar.

"He's mayor of Dodge City now. He'll be governor soon's I bring you back."

"He's a rotten crook. He killed my mom and dad, stole our land, and now he's got a bum warrant out for me in Kansas."

Brady came out of his office, stood off to the side, and watched the two men face off.

It was as if someone had thrown a sizzling stick of dynamite into the saloon. Silence. A standoff at the bar.

"You say that, but you're lyin' like a rug, Slade."

Holiday was loose. He leaned into the bar on one elbow and relaxed. Two miners fled to the corner, near the poker tables.

"I'll have a shot of Jose Cuervo," Holiday said to the bartender.

Bill, the apron, set him up and Holiday chugged it down.

More silence. Like ice melting. The two men eyed each other.

"I'm waitin'," Slade said.

Holiday smiled. "I'm in no hurry. Thought I'd hang around for a while, let you wonder when I'll be comin' for you."

He tipped the bottle of tequila, poured another shot, drank it, and walked back toward the door.

Strong move, Slade thought. Guts.

Slade could have shot Holiday in the back, but then Holiday knew he wouldn't pull a cowardly trick like that.

SLADE

Holiday pushed through the bat-wing doors. Slade quickly followed. He wasn't going to let Holiday dictate the gunfight to him. That was a loser's game.

Holiday was walking down the sidewalk when Slade came out of the saloon. The miners, the game managers, the players, the girls, all followed.

Slade moved out to the middle of the street.

"Holiday!" he yelled.

Jubal turned, smiled, stepped off the board sidewalk, his muscular frame illuminated in the dim glow of the naphtha lamps.

Then Slade saw Johnny Wade. Wade moved out from the other side of the street and stood cocky, confident, all in black, no hat.

"Yeah?" Jubal said.

Brady pushed through the mob circling the street, got himself out front where he had a good view. Calla Carlson moved around to the other side where she could see what was happening.

A stinging jab of anxiety cut through Slade. Two against one. He didn't recognize Johnny Wade, had never seen him before, but he knew instinctively he was with Jubal and that told him something about Holiday.

He regained his composure and pulled a bag of Durham from his shirt pocket, rolled a cigarette, then stuffed the bag back as he silently thanked the old gunsmith in Rapid City who had made the batch of nitrate caps for him.

Slade managed to cuddle the cap with his little finger against his palm as he pulled his hand out of his pocket. He lit the cigarette and took a drag.

"It'll be now. There'll be no waitin', Holiday," Slade said.

"Then I'm officially chargin' you with bank robbery and murder in Dodge City, Kansas. You can come back with me and face the charges . . . or you can take a bullet in the gullet right now, and I'll have you shipped back."

"You talk too goddamn much, Holiday," Slade said. He brought his right hand to his mouth, the nitrate cap still clutched in his fingers. He touched the fuse to the cigarette.

Holiday's hands, his fingers itchy, hung over his holster.

Slade pitched the cigarette at Johnny Wade and at the same time lofted the nitrate cap at the young gunfighter.

His aim was perfect.

The tiny thimble of destruction thumped in front of Johnny Wade. The explosion skied him backward into the seed tore. Slade dipped to one knee, swiveled his Peacemaker from the slot on his gun belt, and fired at Holiday, whose attention had been diverted by the loud blast and the pieces of Johnny Wade that had landed around him. By the time Jubal gripped his gun, three slugs had punctured a neat triangle in his chest.

Jubal fell to his knees. "Shit!" he groaned.

His gun dipped. He pumped bullets into the dirt.

"No, not like this," he whispered.

He fired two more slugs into the street, then bounced forward, and his left arm slid out in front of him. The gun dropped from his right hand.

Johnny Wade's short gunslinging career was over. What was left of his body was scattered in a mass of bloody parts on the sidewalk and street in front of the seed store.

Slade walked forward.

Holiday was still alive.

Silver Creek had never known such a moment and never would again. The crowd stood stiff and silent. Some people, those who liked violence, had sick smiles on their twisted faces.

Slade kicked Holiday's gun away, hooked his boot toe under Jubal's shoulder and rolled him. Blood trickled from the old gunfighter's mouth. His eyes were wide open.

"This is Jubal Holiday, ladies and gentlemen!" Slade shouted. "He came to Silver Creek to die."

"Please, shoot me," Jubal whispered. Blood gurgled from his mouth.

Slade leveled his .45 at Holiday and fired off another shot that tunneled into Jubal's heart.

Holiday shook like Denise had the night before, then lay silent, his career, his legend ended.

Slade dropped his Peacemaker and it swung back into place on his swivel rig. He turned and walked back toward the Regal. The crowd parted for him.

Bill ran into the saloon. He knew Slade would want a drink. He lifted a bottle of Sweet Home from the shelf and sat it on the bar with a shot glass.

Slade poured and drank.

Brady rushed in. He slipped up to the bar and motioned for Bill. Bill brought another glass.

The crowd filed in. The professor slid behind the piano and banged out the first verse of "It's a Good Life."

"You amaze me, Slade," Brady said.

Slade had another drink and ignored his boss.

"There's some kid out there . . . well, he ain't a kid anymore. There's part of a young kid, I'll put it that way, all over the street. How the hell did you do that, Slade?''

A pudgy man with a star pinned to his shirt walked up to Slade and Brady. "Should I get a statement, Mr. Brady? About the gunfight?"

"Oh, Jesus, Jake, forget it, fill something out on your own and get back to your office. Don't bother Slade here with that crap."

The sheriff backed up, then hurried out of the saloon.

"So, that's the sheriff here in Silver Creek," Slade said.

Brady smiled. "My sheriff. Don't worry about him. He does what he's told. He didn't hear anything about warrants for you in Kansas. I'll see to that."

Slade's body was shimmering with a nervous tremble, not unlike the buzz a man gets when he's just raked in a pot of money in a big stakes poker game.

"Goddamn, Slade, what was that thing you blew the kid up with?" Brady asked.

"A little secret of mine."

Brady shook his head with disbelief. "The kid, he was with Holiday, wasn't he? It was two on one, right?"

Slade nodded. "Would you have some of your men pick up the remains, put them in boxes, and ship them to Mr. Cliff Langdon, Dodge City, Kansas?"

"Anything you say, Slade."

"I'd appreciate that."

"And why don't you take the night off. Hell, take tomorrow off too, Slade."

Slade saw Calla Carlson standing near the poker tables. She looked away when their eyes met.

"Sure." Slade smiled. "I wouldn't mind havin' some time off, Mr. Brady."

"Absolutely. A man like you around the Regal will be great for business. Just great."

Slade walked slowly toward the bat-wing doors.

"Slade!"

Slade turned. "What is it, Brady?" he snapped.

"I'm willing to make you a better deal too."

A better deal? Slade wished he could get a better deal from life, but he knew the Holiday incident was just another link in the chain of cause and effect that locked him inexorably into a life on the run.

Slade walked out into the street and ambled over to Holiday. He knelt, lifted the badge from Jubal's shirt.

He wanted to send the marshal's star back to Cliff Langdon personally.

Chapter Twenty-five

Slade was thankful for the time off. It gave him a chance to work on a plan to break Calla and the others girls out of the Regal.

He stripped down to his shorts and lay on his bed at the Wheeler House. At least now Holiday was no longer a problem, no longer on his mind.

Slade thought it over. He'd take the girls out by going in shooting, then he'd put them on the stage to Bozeman and ride with Calla back to Miles City. There was a stage due tomorrow afternoon. He could put his plan into effect after the girls came in from their Sunday outing.

Slade washed up and went out to eat, but before he stopped at a café, he walked to the livery stable. By now word of the gunfight had spread through Silver Creek like news of a new strike.

Hank, the owner, perked up when he saw Slade. He

stuck out his hand. "That was mighty fine shootin' this evening, Mr. Slade. I'm proud to know you."

"I'll be needin' a horse," Slade said.

"Got a roan, got a Morgan, got that mare over there."

"No mares, too damn temperamental for me, Hank. Besides, they're quitters."

Slade checked out the Morgan, felt his legs, checked the shoes, his mouth and eyes. A good strong horse, very healthy. The Morgan would ride Calla to Miles City easily.

"I'll take the Morgan," Slade said.

Hank smiled, saw dollar signs. "It's a sixty-dollar horse, Mr. Slade."

"I'll need a saddle too."

"Got a new Brooks, a Brazos, a Nelson."

"Need one with a high cantle."

Again Hank smiled. "A woman gonna be usin' it, huh? Make it easy on her back. I'd take that Brooks there, got a nice high lady-cantle on it."

"I'm pickin' up a lady from the stage tomorrow. She'll want a horse, a good saddle," Slade lied.

"Sure, sure, I understand," Hank said.

"And, Hank, I'd like to keep this quiet, real quiet," Slade said, his voice firm with a hard edge.

Hank got the point. "My mouth's closed, Mr. Slade."

Hank's son, Billy, had been watching from a stall. Slade turned to him. "Billy, you go to the store and get me a bedroll, waterproof tarp, couple quilts sewn between patched overcoats. Need a couple blankets, a roll, an oil slicker. I want to outfit my horse and the lady's horse."

He handed Billy two gold coins.

"You bet, Mr. Slade. I'll have everything ready."

"Than you'll be needin' your Appaloosa and the Morgan tomorrow?" Hank said.

"Need my horse in the morning, the Morgan near stage time in the afternoon."

"We'll have everything prepared, Mr. Slade," Hank said.

Slade pushed a stack of gold coins into Hank's hand. "And I meant what I said about keepin' this quiet. You talk and you end up like Holiday."

Hank stiffened. "Aw, now, no need for that. I'm a businessman, Mr. Slade. I'll do as you say."

Slade relaxed and smiled. "Good. See to it that everything's ready for me tomorrow. And thanks."

Slade left the stable and ate dinner. He walked to the Regal, had a drink, and motioned Calla over.

"It'll be tomorrow. Tell the ladies, make sure everyone's ready by stage time at three. They'll be leavin' for Bozeman if everything works. We'll head for Miles City."

Calla nodded and quickly walked to some men at the chuck-a-luck.

Slade finished his drink, then took a stroll along Silver Creek. He moved slowly near the rushing stream, thinking about his life, what he would do after he got Calla back to Miles City . . . if indeed he could pull off everything he had planned.

The next morning Slade rode along the stream, past the mesas, with the mountains on the other side, out into the valley, and down into the mining district.

He found Caleb's cabin. Denise was walking around from the back with a pail of water.

"Slade!" she yelled.

"I've come to talk with your father."

Denise set the pail on the porch. "And not me?" she said, slapping her hands to her hips, standing in a challenging pose, elbows hooked out.

"Came to see you too, Denise."

Caleb appeared at the front door. "What the hell are you doin' here, Slade? We don't want you around."

"Give him a chance to talk, Pa," Denise said.

"What you think and what actually's been happenin' are two things," Slade said, his words just as icy and distant as Caleb's greeting.

Slade dismounted and strode into the cabin. Mary was frying bacon and the place smelled like breakfast.

Caleb followed Slade in. "You turned on us. We thought you were gonna help."

Slade sat down. Caleb took a chair across from him, and Denise slipped into the chair next to Slade. "Just listen to Slade, Daddy."

Caleb ignored his lovely young daughter. "We heard about the gunfight, heard how you killed a marshal, how you're wanted for murder and robbery."

Mary cracked some eggs on the edge of the frying pan and fried them in the bacon grease. Then she set a plate in front of Caleb.

"Give Slade some breakfast too, Mama," Denise said.

Mary looked at Caleb. He said, "No. I won't eat with a killer and crook."

Slade lifted a cheroot from his jeans pocket and lit it without asking permission, then he told his story about Kansas, about Carlson back in Miles City, about Calla, and about his plan to free her and the other girls from Brady.

"I told you." Denise smiled. Then she added, "But, Slade, you didn't tell me about Kansas, about your ma and pa."

Caleb gave his daughter a disapproving glance. "When have you been conversing with Mr. Slade?" he asked.

Slade didn't let her answer. "My suggestion is for you to hire Pringle. Let him chart the veins for the association, and when this area plays out, take him with you, do what Brady did, use the vein law in your favor. It's legal, and Pringle knows how to apply it."

Mary set a plate of steaming eggs and bacon in front of Slade.

Caleb scratched his beard. "Not a bad idea, Slade. Sorry, guess I had you pegged wrong."

"Tomorrow I'll go up against Brady and his men. If my plan works, you'll be free of him."

"But if it doesn't . . ." Caleb whispered.

"You'll need help, Slade," Denise put in. "The miners can go up against Brady with you."

"Please, Miz Denise, let me do it my way. You yourself said none of the miners can use a gun to any advantage."

Denise nodded, then looked quickly at her father. Caleb stared back at his daughter with a stern look. "You two have been seein' each other?" he asked.

Mary set a cup of coffee in front of Slade. "It's obvious they know each other, Caleb," she said, "and I have no problem about it."

"But, but . . ." Caleb lamented.

Again, Slade took control. "Your daughter is a fine young woman, Caleb. She cares about you, about her mother, about the miners' association. We've talked, that's all," he lied.

"Well, I . . ."

"Daddy, stop. I'm old enough to hold my own now."

Slade looked at Caleb. It was obvious. Denise had been right. He was dying, anyone could see that, maybe even his wife.

"Tomorrow, if I succeed, you should be rid of Brady," Slade said.

"We owe you," Caleb confessed.

"There was talk about a payment. I'll take that if things go okay tomorrow, just before the stage for Bozeman leaves. Could you have it ready?"

"I can bring it to him," Denise said to Caleb.

Caleb relaxed. He smiled, gave his daughter an appreciative frown. "Okay, okay. I'll have the money ready tomorrow, and Denise can ride in with it. But what if you don't succeed, Slade?"

Slade finished his breakfast, leaned back, and sighed. "I'd like Miz Denise to bury me and say a few words over my dirt."

He got up and walked out of the cabin. Denise followed. Slade mounted the Appaloosa.

Denise reached up and touched his thigh. "I'll be there tomorrow when the stage pulls in. I'll have your money. Can we talk then?"

Slade looked down at the pretty young lass. "Only if you tell me how old you are," he said.

Denise curled her lips, her chin jutted out, her green eyes flashed. "You worry too much about that, Slade," she said, then slapped his Appaloosa on the ass, sending the big animal off toward the creek.

Chapter Twenty-six

A hot afternoon blasted Silver Creek when the girls returned from their Sunday outing. Slade rode behind them into town.

Summer had set in. A hot wind out of the Gallatin Valley blew circles of dust along the main street.

Slade went to his room at the Wheeler House, packed his gear, tied it up, and slung it over his shoulder. He walked the back streets to the livery stable. He had to hurry now if he was to break the girls out in time to catch the stage for Bozeman.

All the guards knew him; that would be in his favor. They would be off balance . . . at least at first. He found Hank and his son at the stable, left his possibles with them, and walked into the alley behind the saloon with his Winchester rifle.

The guards in the alley greeted him. "Hi, Slade. What's up?"

Slade walked up to the nearest guard and slammed the barrel of his rifle into his neck. The guard went down. Slade banged the stock into the man's chin and took him out.

The other guard stiffened. "Hey, shit, Slade. What the hell's goin' on?"

Slade cocked the rifle. The guard went for his gun. Slade walked forward, pulled the trigger, hit him once in the belly; another slug dug into his chest. The guard fell to one knee. Slade cocked the lever and pushed another shell into the chamber as the man tipped over into the dust.

They'd hear the shots inside. Slade knew the back door was locked, bolted. He rushed around to the front of the saloon and busted through the bat-wing doors. Bill the bartender looked up.

"Keep steady, Bill. Stay where you are and you'll be fine."

Bill nodded and Slade headed up the stairs to the suites.

The first guard, a tall, lanky cowboy, came to the head of the stairs and blocked Slade's way. "Brady didn't say you were comin' up, Slade."

Slade kept coming. The guard's hand lifted and hung above his holster.

"I'm taking the girls," Slade said.

"No, not without Brady's permission!"

Slade blasted the young dude with his Winchester, levered it and fired again. The guard rolled past him down the steps. The other guard ran down the hall, a double-barreled shotgun blasting. Slade hit the top of the stairs and flew forward, skidding on his belly. The buckshot whizzed over his head.

The cowboy pulled a Navy Special and fired. Slade rolled to one side, hit the wall, came up on one knee, and cracked off three quick shots. The man stumbled, clutched at the banister, then somersaulted over it and smashed into a poker table below.

"All right, ladies!" Slade yelled.

The suite doors opened simultaneously. The girls were dressed in traveling clothes and carried bags.

One of Brady's best men took a position behind an overturned poker table down in the saloon area and hammered off two shots into the hallway. Slade herded the girls into Calla's room.

"Wait here!" he shouted.

He hit the floor again, crawled on his belly back out into the hall. Bullets sprayed the wall above him. Slade moved to the stair railing and fired three shots at the poker table.

No response.

According to his count—but he could be wrong—Slade had five shots left in his rifle.

"I'll blow you and half the saloon away!" Slade hollered. "Just like I did to the kid with Holiday!"

The Regal was empty now. Those miners and drinkers, the gamblers, who had watched the beginning of the escape had all scampered through the bat-wing doors.

Brady's man behind the poker table lifted up. He dropped his Henry rifle. Slade called to the girls. They walked down the stairs ahead of him. He watched the man behind the poker table, saw his hand go limp, knew immediately he was going for a vest gun. Slade blasted him with two quick shots from the Winchester.

Brady rushed out of his office. His fingernails dug into his cheek. "What the . . . what's going on out here, Slade? What's this all about?"

"I'm takin' the ladies out of here."

Brady was stunned. His gaze turned from one dead body to the other.

"I'm freein' the girls," Slade said, ushering the women down the long, spiral staircase.

Brady ran to his office. Slade and the girls came to the bottom of the stairs. Brady bolted back out with an old Hawken rifle that looked as though it would blow up in his face if he fired it.

He was nervous, his body trembled, and it was obvious he wanted to scratch his face, but he lifted the antique gun and pointed it at the girls. "I'll kill the first woman who tries to leave!"

"Put that thing away, Brady, before you hurt yourself. You don't know anything about guns."

Brady's hands trembled. "I can't believe you'd do this to me, Slade, not after what I've done for you, taking you in, giving you a good job."

Slade smiled. "Just proves you can't trust anyone."

Brady tried to fire the gun.

Nothing.

Slade walked over and disarmed him.

"You kidnapped these young women, Brady. That's a federal crime."

A young redheaded girl who worked the suites came up to Slade. "May I have your pistol, Mr. Slade?" she asked, then lifted it from Slade's holster. She pointed the gun at Brady.

Brady backed up until he was halfway into his office.

The redhead followed, cocking the hammer of the big Peacemaker, holding it in both hands.

"You are a despicable man, Brady. You're not even a man. You're an animal. You've kept us prisoner, you've beaten us. You've ruined us. We'll never be the same."

"Now, look, I was just countin' the week's take. You girls can have the money on my desk. I was gonna pay you. Take all this money on my desk. I was gonna pay all of you soon. I would have let you go."

Gold, silver, greenbacks were stacked neatly on Brady's big desk.

The little redhead moved forward, still pointing the gun. Brady backstepped until he bumped into the desk. She pulled the trigger and hit him in the shoulder.

"Owww!" he screeched.

The redhead clicked the hammer and shot again. This time she sent a slug into Brady's belly. It opened his vest. Blood spewed. His eyes bulged. He stared for a moment at the girl. She smiled. Brady looked past her to Slade, turned, tried to grab the edge of his desk, then slumped to the floor.

The girls burst into a loud round of applause and cheered. They laughed as Brady struggled to pull himself up against the desk.

The redhead shot again and hit him in the back, and he spilled to the floor. The girl walked forward, stood over Brady, her hands shaking.

Slade walked into Brady's office and checked the crooked kidnapper. "Dead as a fall leaf," he said.

The girls were still clapping.

Slade turned to them. "I think you ladies are entitled

to this money, but hurry, we have a stagecoach to catch.''

The girls gathered around the desk.

Sid Pringle walked in. "What's happened here?'' he asked calmly.

Slade took his gun from the redhead, pointed it at Pringle. "You're workin' for a new boss. You best ride out to Crooked Valley and offer your services to the miners first thing tomorrow.''

Pringle looked past Slade at Brady, than at the girls, and watched as they filled their traveling bags with money. The redhead knelt in front of Brady's safe, scooping coins into an open umbrella.

"You kill him?'' Pringle asked.

"No, one of the women did.''

"I've done nothing illegal,'' Pringle said. "I worked a legal law.''

"That you did. Now go work for the miners. The gulch will play out soon. You owe them.''

"That's fine with me, Slade. I'm a geologist. I work at mining. I don't care for whom I work as long as I'm paid well.''

"If you don't go to work for the miners, don't do a good job, don't stay with them until the law is changed, I'll come back for you, Pringle.''

Pringle backed up. "As I said, sir, I'm a professional. I'll see the miners first thing tomorrow.''

Slade followed him out into the saloon. Pringle turned and left. Bill was wiping the bar nervously out of habit.

"Jeez, Slade, what about me?''

"Looks like you got yourself a saloon here, Bill. You'll run a clean place, right?''

"Me? Mine?"

"Why not? Who else?"

Again, out of habit, Bill put up a bottle of Sweet Home and a glass.

"I'll pass this time, Bill," Slade said.

The women filed out of Brady's office. Slade led them out of the saloon, down the street, past the sidewalks filled with gawkers, to the stage. The girls lined up and one by one shook Slade's hand, pecked him on the cheek, and handed him a fistful of greenbacks.

Slade nodded to each one. "Much obliged, ma'am."

Slade held the door open and helped the ladies into the stage. "This'll take you to Bozeman, from there you're on you're own."

The stage cut curls in the dusty street as it lumbered north out of town. Slade turned and saw Brady's hand-picked sheriff standing nervously across the street.

Slade reloaded his Peacemaker and walked toward him. "You can leave if you'll get out of town right now."

"I never did like it much here," the fat man said. He took his badge off, threw it by a water barrel, and walked down the street.

"If you don't leave, the miners will see to you!" Slade yelled after him.

He walked back to Calla and they went to the livery stable.

Denise was waiting for him. She looked beautiful, in a stunning black dress, black boots, and a black hat propped fetchingly on her head.

"Go on in and I'll be along in a minute," Slade told Calla.

Then he walked over to Denise.

"Well?" she said.

Slade smiled. "Well?"

"I guess this ends it."

Slade nodded.

"I won't have to kill you after all." Denise chuckled.

"I'm thankful for that, Denise."

"Will you ever go back to Kansas, Slade? Try and clear your name?"

"Not as long as Langdon is alive, and it looks like he'll be runnin' Kansas soon."

Denise held out an envelope. "Here's your money from the miners."

"I won't be needin' that. You keep it, Denise. Keep it for yourself. The ladies from the saloon gave me quite a stake, and I got a big payoff waitin' for me in Miles City from Mr. Carlson. I want you to have that money."

"But Slade—"

"Take it. You deserve it. You did as much as anyone to save the association. Make sure you daddy is comfortable before he . . . before . . ."

"He dies?"

"And then, after things are going straight and good here, you and your ma can go somewhere, start over by yourselves."

"I'm never gonna forget you, Frank Slade."

"I can say the same, Denise."

Denise looked down one end of Main Street, then the other, and finally up at Slade. "I'll see you again, Slade. The West ain't that big."

"Not with you in it." Slade smiled.

Denise pushed up on the toes of her boots, hooked

her arms around Slade, and kissed him. Then she turned and walked away.

Slade watched. "Denise!" he yelled.

She turned. "Yeah?"

"How old are you?"

"Old enough to have married you, Frank Slade," Denise shouted back, then turned again and walked like a woman to her horse.

Chapter Twenty-seven

Slade and Calla camped along the Yellowstone River their first night out. Before the sun went down Slade waded out into the river and trapped two big trout, brought them back, and cleaned them. They cooked the fish over hot coals.

"Who was that girl at the stable?" Calla asked.

"Her name was Denise."

"How did you know her?"

Slade didn't feel like a question-and-answer session about Denise, so he cut it short. "It's none of your business, Calla."

"I'm sorry."

They sat in silence for a few minutes, then Slade laid out the blankets and quilts. Calla kept her riding clothes on and slipped in. Slade sat at the fire.

"Come sleep with me," Calla said.

Slade got up, poured some coffee over the coals, and joined Calla. He slid under the covers next to her.

"I've thought a lot about getting back to Miles City. I think there's a real future there," Calla whispered.

"It's a new town, a cattle town. It'll be there for a long time."

"I can make the hotel something really fine."

"You'll do well."

"But will I ever get over what has happened to me?"

"You will because you have to, Miz Carlson."

"I suppose."

Slade fired a cheroot. Calla's hand crept to his thigh. "I still remember that night you came to my suite at the Regal."

Slade said, "So do I."

"Would you like to finish that?"

"I'd like to, but it wouldn't be right. I'm workin' for your father. It wouldn't be right."

Calla's hand caressed between his legs.

Slade removed it.

"You're serious?" Calla said.

"It's like I said."

"I respect that, Slade," Calla said.

The trip to Miles City was uneventful. Carlson was elated with Slade's success and delighted to see his daughter again. After the reunion, Slade collected his fee, and stayed over in the Carlson House.

Carlson came to his room late.

"I paid you, but I didn't say thank you properly. Getting my daughter back was the most important thing in life to me."

"That's easy to understand," Slade said.

"There's some news about the Taylor woman, the woman who stole your money."

"Yes?"

"She's down in the Dakota Territory, the Black Hills, place called Lead."

"I know the town," Slade said. "Right next to Deadwood."

Carlson took a chair. "They're still mining gold out of the gulch, and this woman is working in a saloon there."

"Thanks for the information."

"I felt like I owed it to you. But listen, Slade, you got a good stake, it might be best to let it be."

"Might," Slade murmured.

He lay on the bed in a fresh pair of balbriggans, smoking the stub of a cigar. The laughter and howls of the drunken soldiers from Fort Keogh lifted through the open window.

"Calla told me what happened."

"It's been a long, tiresome trip, Mr. Carlson."

"She told me how you respected her."

Silence.

Carlson got up. "Well, I'll be leavin' now."

Slade rose from the bed and shook the old man's hand.

"My daughter's all I had left in life, Slade. Thanks."

"She'll need time to get over what's happened to her," Slade said.

"I realize that, but she's strong. She'll be okay."

"Yes, of course she will," Slade said. "She'll need me. It's not pretty what she's been through, any of those girls. The scar went so deep one of them killed Brady."

"I know, Calla told me the story. Where to now,

Slade?'' Carlson walked to the door, stopped, waite
for an answer.

"I'm thinkin' on that, Mr. Carlson."

Carlson smiled and left, closing the door softly.

Slade lay back on the bed with a bottle of Swee
Home. He clutched the neck, tipped the bottle, and gu
gled down a strong shot.

The whiskey filtered through him. He breathed deeply
Closed his eyes. He studied his situation. The key wa
staying ahead of Langdon and the phony charges in Kar
sas. Langdon would never give up. Slade knew that b
now. There would be more Jubal Holidays, more Johnn
Wades.

He reached back and pinched his shoulder blades
working his fingers in a slow massage, untying the knot
of tension. He slid another shot of Sweet Home dow
into his belly and fired up a cheroot.

A soft knock on his door jolted Slade out of the bed
He grabbed his rifle, cocked it, and waited.

Again the knock.

"Who is it?"

"It's Calla, Slade. May I come in?"

Slade got up and opened the door. Calla swayed i
wearing a silky black dressing gown that flapped fror
her sides like butterfly wings as she walked. Her blon
hair was brushed out full and natural, scooped back o
the top of her head, along her temples, then flushing ou
like speckles of fine gold on her shoulders.

She sat down on the bed and crossed her legs, showe
Slade a pair of new black laced boots.

"Drink?" Slade offered.

"Sure."

Frank poured two, handed her a glass. Calla sippe

ightly. Slade leaned against the wall by the window. He
uffed his cheroot. The thick gray cloud of smoke fun-
eled out over the street below.

"Now that things are over, your job is done, and
ou've been compensated—I thought now perhaps you'd
et me thank you for what you did."

"Aww, that's not necessary."

"Oh, but it is, Slade."

She was stunningly beautiful in the glow of the coal
il lamp.

"Just forget it."

"Oh, God, Slade," Calla whispered. "Don't you un-
lerstand? This is for me more than you."

"For you?"

"All those days in the Regal, all the men. I've be-
:ome jaded, cold. It's like someone stole a piece of me,
in invisible piece. I want that piece of me back. If I can
ossibly get it back. I might be too far gone, but I don't
vant to be. I want to enjoy love. I want to feel good
ibout sex. I have to know how it's going to be now. I'm
ittracted to you . . . I have to see what will happen. Do
ou understand?"

Slade did of course. Especially the part about the piece
of her that had been stolen. He'd been robbed of his
freedom.

"Sure, I understand," Slade said.

He set his glass down and came to the bed, slid an
arm around Calla's waist, and tenderly pulled her back.

She lay supine, the black gown falling open, framing
he alabaster white of her gorgeous body. Her hair flowed
out behind her on the pillow.

Slade stood over the bed. He took his shorts down,

stripped naked, and sat on the bed. Calla offered her hand.

He took it, held it, their fingers entwining, squeezing, talking. Slade bent over and kissed her gently. Her lips tasted like redberry wine.

Her hand found his stiff erection. Her fingers fluttered up and down the billowing stalk. She lifted herself off the bed, sat up, then bent over Slade and took him in her mouth.

Her blond hair splashed on his thighs like sand. Her mouth was warm, bubbly. Slade relaxed, leaned back on the bed. Calla's head bobbed up and down.

Slade finally grabbed her shoulders and lifted her off. She lay back on the bed, shaking the black gown off. Slade kissed her thighs, her belly, his tongue circling her belly button, then dipping lower.

"Ohhhh, jeeezzuzzz, Slade," Calla moaned.

Frank pleasured her, making sure he was going at it slowly, working with her, bringing her along.

Calla cocked her knees apart. Slade lowered himself on top of her. She reached out and fisted his cock, pulled him down, put him in.

Slade stroked her. Calla lay beneath him stiff, tense. Frank sawed slower, slower, slower, until Calla wrapped her arms around his shoulders and banged up against him, rolling gently, screwing Slade deeper into her wetness.

Frank worked harder. Calla held on as if that piece of her she had lost had been resurrected. Her body vibrated. She had a joyous expression etched on her beautiful face.

"Yes, Slade. Yes! Give to back to me. Make me

hole, Slade! Make me whole . . . make me . . . ah, hhh, Slade!''

Calla's words were like hot bullets in the night. Slade cked faster. She scissored her legs around him . . . iffened . . . shuddered. She pumped quick jabs at lade. He hammered back at her.

The healing came in a brilliant explosion of emotion d passion. Slade couldn't remember what Calla said him. He was deaf to the real world, consumed by a nging, a harmony, a moment out of time.

Slade did hear Calla moments later as they lay beside ach other. ''I'm okay now, Slade. I know I am. Thank ou.''

Slade didn't know what to say, so he kept quiet.

Calla finally got up, pulled on the gown, and turned Slade. She bent over and kissed him. ''I had to find ut. You understand, don't you? See if I could be . . . it could be . . . like before . . . before Brady.''

''Yes,'' Frank said.

''You're a good man, Slade. Come back and see me omeday. Will you?''

''That would be a pleasure.''

She smiled. ''You'll be on the move now?''

''In a few hours.''

''I shudder to think what would have happened if you adn't come through Miles City in the first place, Slade. ate is funny, isn't it?''

Frank Slade's wound was fate. Lady Fortuna's wheel ad taken a wicked spin and landed on him, picked him ut as a young boy, set the rules, dealt the cards he'd ave to play.

Why?

Frank asked himself that question as he saddled hi Appaloosa late that night after seeing Calla.

"Slade! Slade!"

The old man from the Western Union office came puf ing into the livery stable. "Glad I caught you, Mr. Slade This just come for you." He handed Frank an envelope

Slade tore it open and read.

IF YOU'RE INTERESTED IN ROBBIN'
A BANK FOR A GOOD CAUSE
COME SEE ME RITE AWAY.
BLACK HILLS . . . FRENCH CREEK.
CALAMITY JANE

Frank slipped out of town under a bright moon th cast a silvery shimmer over the prairie. He leaned fo ward in the saddle, his feet solid in the stirrups, an headed southeast out of Miles City toward Dakota Te ritory.

Epilogue

Pretty LaRue leaned toward Cliff Langdon's desk. Her small, solid body looked fetching in the red evening dress, the bodice lifting her supple breasts into a heaving cleavage.

Her black hair had been brushed back and off to the side to enhance her pale, smooth face. Her deep, brown eyes flashed passion and intrigue as she stared at Langdon.

Langdon smiled. "I've heard a lot about you, Miss LaRue."

"Probably not as much as I've heard about you," she shot back, lifting a glass of whiskey from the edge of his desk.

"Heard about you, Slade, and the Pueblo Kid, the shoot-out in Horseshoe Springs, how you nursed them both back to health."

Pretty tipped the drink and took it down, then leaned back in the plush leather chair and crossed her legs.

"Didn't do much good. Slade killed Pueblo later outside Deadwood."

"Sent me his marshal's badge. Sent me the badge pinned on Jubal Holiday too."

Pretty smiled. "He's a tough one."

"I want him," Langdon said sternly. "I want him badly, Miss LaRue. I'm prepared to offer you a deal that could make you a rich lady."

"I'm listening."

"You know Slade better than I do. I saw him only for a few minutes." Langdon drew a finger along a deep scar on his face. "He did this. You see my face? He ruined it. I'm ugly. He did it to me."

"And?"

"I brought you here from Denver because I think you can bring Slade back to Kansas."

"How?" Pretty asked.

"I've sent two of the best gunmen in the West against him. They're both dead. You figure a way."

"Me?"

"As I understand it, you were his lover in Horseshoe Flats."

"You want me to bring him back to Dodge City?"

"That's right, Miss LaRue, and if you do you'll live a fine life until you die. I'll draw up a contract."

Pretty watched the rich banker finger his scars. His eyes were intense.

"A woman stole his money. She was the sheriff's wife up in a place called Sand Springs, Montana Territory. She's working a saloon in the Black Hills. I figure Slade

ill visit her. He'll be back in Dakota soon. That's the
ay I see it.''

''You draw up that contract, Mr. Langdon, and if it's
my liking, I'll get Slade back here for you.''

A big smile wrinkled into Langdon's scars. ''That's
hat I wanted to hear. I don't care how you do it, just
et the job done. He'll never suspect you, he'll be off
uard.''

Pretty poured a drink, sipped at it. ''Slade's got flaws.
e's too sentimental when it comes to women. You draw
p the contract and I'll come up with a plan. I'll need
couple men. You have an under-sheriff here in Dodge
amed Bat Masterson?''

''Yes, signed on a couple months ago. Very impres-
ve. He's young, fast, and nothing scares him.''

''I want Masterson,'' Pretty said. ''I'll need his
elp.''

''Good choice, Miss LaRue. I didn't think of Master-
on for this job.''

''It's because he could never take Slade alone. He'll
eed me as much as I'll need him.''

''Anything, anything you want, you need. Slade has
ecome an embarrassment to me. I can't run for gov-
nor until I finish this, do you understand?''

Pretty got up. Landgon appraised her body, the way
rippled against the tight red dress.

She stuck out her hand. ''I'll finish it for you, Mr.
angdon. You can count on bein' governor, but it's
nna cost you.''

Langdon smiled. ''That, my dear, is the least of my
orries.''

He stood up, took Pretty's hand, and kissed her fin-
rs.

Watch for

Return to Dodge City

*next in the Slade series
coming soon
from Lynx!*